WILL POOLE'S ISLAND

Will Poole's Island

TIM WEED

South Hampton, New Hampshire

Library of Congress Control Number: 2013957898

ISBN 978-1-60898-173-1 (hardcover: alk. paper)
ISBN 978-1-60898-174-8 (paperback: alk. paper)
ISBN 978-1-60898-175-5 (ebook)

www.namelos.com

for John Alonzo Edwards

One

April 1643

His Majesty's Connecticut Colonies

Will Poole's bed had grown smaller overnight. The planks above the straw mattress were lower than he remembered, and the timber rail that kept him from rolling out of the low-ceilinged loft seemed closer. The bricks of the chimney wall, still warm from last night's fire, pressed against his right thigh and shoulder. The truth was, the whole house had come to feel intolerably cramped of late. Fumbling his way around in the darkness, he pulled on breeches, doublet, garters, and shoes and crept down the ladder. If he hurried, he might be able to reach the outdoors undetected. At the hearth, he put his hand into the pot suspended over the whitened ashes for a handful of corn bannock. He chewed quickly, wiping his hand on his breeches before reaching up to ease his father's old snaphaunce musket down from its pegs above the mantel. He threw the powder horn and shot bag over his shoulder and crept toward the door, wincing as his cautious steps made the floorboards creak. His hand was on the latch when the voice he'd been dreading froze him in place.

"Where to, Will?"

Will turned to face his guardian, James Overlock. "To the forest."

"If it's venison you want, we can buy it from the savages for a string of beads."

After Will's father's death last October, Overlock, the family servant, had been declared Will's legal guardian. Though it was still before dawn, the plump Yorkshireman had donned his leather apron, which indicated that he'd already been up for some time. Will hesitated, torn between an irresistible urge to escape and a lifelong habit of obedience.

"Don't be a child, Will. Leave the hunting to the savages. I can't tend to your family's fortunes alone, you know."

Will shifted the heavy musket from one hand to the other. The house reeked of onions, cinders, and months of close living. It had been a cold winter, with endless snowstorms and bitter winds that had kept the two of them inside at all hours, shivering by the hearth. Now spring was here. Will's desire to be outdoors—outside the house, outside the fortified wall that enclosed this colonial outpost—was as palpable as a toothache. "The Governor has offered a gold double crown for the head of a certain black she-wolf," he pointed out. "Wouldn't *that* tend to our fortunes more than turning the soil or repairing the roof?"

The steward smiled. "It seems unlikely you would be able to track down such a beast, Will, when dozens of more experienced men have failed. Do you think you can just saunter out and shoot it?"

"With the Lord's blessing, perhaps, should He see fit to grant it ... " Will trailed off, embarrassed by his own insincere piety. He wasn't even sure he *believed* in the Lord, though he would never be so foolish as to admit it.

"You're not a boy anymore, Will. The moment has come to start acting like a man."

Now Will felt anger rising. James Overlock's face was more familiar to him than almost any other—well-fed, balding, cheeks like smooth red apples above a black beard trimmed to a fastidious point in the style of the famous portraits of King Charles by Anthony van Dyck—and he'd come to detest the very sight of it. Yet he had to be careful. Overlock had been his father's trusted steward, the only servant of the dozens previously attached to the Poole household chosen to accompany the family to America. Upon his father's death, Overlock had taken on the legal rights of a parent. On a whim, he could have Will whipped, flogged, or humiliated in the public stockade. Beyond that, the steward had his plump hands on what remained of the family fortune. Will's brother, Zeke, had made it clear his last time ashore: "You must stay on his good side, Will. You must obey him in all things, though it may pain you to do so. Your future depends on it."

Overlock would find a way to make him suffer for this morning's disobedience, of that Will had no doubt. Still, remaining at home on this spring day was inconceivable. He reached for the latch. "I'm sorry, James, but I really must go. I'll work like a dog tomorrow, I promise."

Outside in the raw morning air, the image of the steward's wide-eyed astonishment lingered in Will's mind. No doubt Overlock's surprise had already changed to fury. And that would change to a calmer and more abiding kind of mood. A mood, Will thought ruefully, that could be altogether more dangerous for his prospects.

Very well. Short of going back in, apologizing, and agreeing to spend the day engaged in household chores—which he had no intention of doing—there was nothing he could do about it. For the rest of the morning at least, he was free. He could worry about Overlock later.

Spirits lifting, he strode along the earthen lane past Widow Benedict's tiny cottage and Goodman Howland's more imposing two-story house. New Meadow, or The New Meadow Plantation and Covenant as it was officially named, consisted of nearly sixty such dwellings—hemlock-beamed English houses sheathed in rough cedar clapboard, most painted blue, some left to weather gray in the salt-laden air. It was spring by the calendar, but the morning was still cold enough that he could see his own breath. In the yards and lanes, last year's grass lay pallid and yellow, like sodden parchment glued to the ground. The smell of rotting compost and soaked ash reached his nostrils. Flocks of migrating geese filled the dawn with their honking.

At the edge of the village lay an open common, close-cropped by livestock, with a few cows and swine loose upon it. Beyond this, protecting the settlement from the wilderness that surrounded it, was the palisade, a massive wall of split logs sharpened on both ends and plunged deep into the earth, one flush against the next. This fortification enclosed the village in the shape of an oblong diamond, with one point left open to the harbor. Square-roofed watchtowers loomed over each of the three landward corners, and a heavy gate of doubled-up hardwood planks bolted together with iron *clavos* provided access during the daylight hours. Passing through this gate, Will nodded to the watchman on duty, who glanced at the boy's musket and raised his eyebrows.

"Going hunting, are ye?"

"I thought I'd give it a try, yes."

"God be with you. I pray your powder is not wasted." The watchman's voice dripped with disapproval. Apparently he shared Overlock's view that a young man's time would more profitably be spent on honest work such as tending to his dwelling place or preparing the ground for crops.

Outside the palisade, the pastures and stubble fields were shrouded in early morning fog. Knee-deep in this dissipating cloud layer, with his late father's musket cradled on his shoulder, Will strode toward the forest with its red-budded canopy swaying and whistling in a gusty breeze. Most of the inhabitants of New Meadow were terrified of the forest. The palisade was a source of comfort, a high barrier keeping the howling beasts and shadowy demons of the wilderness at bay. To Will, lately, the palisade had begun to outweigh the wilderness as an object of dread. It had begun to feel less like a protective fortification and more like the walls of a prison.

He followed the Indian trail north along the river. The wind in the canopy picked up suddenly, rising to a shriek before dying down again, leaving the forest cloaked in haunted silence. Three young deer brandished their white tails like warning flags as they bounded off. He would save his shot for the black she-wolf. Her behavior was akin to a ghost or a hallucination materializing suddenly to prey on the plantation's sheep and swine, then fading back into the forest, leaving neither spoor nor distinguishable tracks. In a grove of stone-grey beech a violent thumping sound caused his heart to skip—but it was only a startled grouse. A moment later he heard footfalls lumbering through last year's papery leaves. He dropped to a crouch and raised the musket, sighting down the barrel in the direction of the footfalls. Whatever it was lurked unseen amidst the beech trunks and the dark green hemlock boughs. Could it be the she-wolf? He held his breath, waiting.

The rustling commenced again, then ceased abruptly as a tiny auburn creature leapt up onto a lichen-covered boulder. Will exhaled, lowering the flintlock. Only a squirrel! Amazing how sounds could be magnified in such a silence. A person heard what he wanted to hear, or what he dreaded, so that even a harmless squirrel could seem as monstrous as a wolf.

Lately, Will had been struggling to separate the real from the imaginary. He'd been experiencing hallucinations. They came to him as daydreams: vivid imaginary scenes that appeared as if they were actually before his eyes. He could be hoeing in the herb garden, and suddenly he would find himself eavesdropping on a conversation in the house of a family he knew or standing on the deserted deck of a sloop anchored in the harbor. He could be sitting in the Meetinghouse and then, suddenly, he would be inside a hearth looking out through crackling flames at someone's disorderly parlor or sitting atop a pine tree at the edge of the forest. The hallucinations came at the most unpredictable moments, in lightning-quick flashes. They never lasted long enough for him to make any sense of them. They frightened him deeply, but he could not, of course, even think about mentioning them to anyone. He could be accused of being demon-possessed, a practitioner of witchcraft, unwitting, perhaps, but mortally dangerous to the community. He could face official scrutiny, imprisonment, public humiliation, or worse.

Morning slipped into afternoon. He wandered, keeping his eyes and ears pricked for signs of the she-wolf. Sometimes he stopped to chew pine pitch or peel a few of last year's beechnuts. Eventually, feeling drowsy, he found a mossy boulder with a good view of any possible line of approach. He unbuckled his oxhide shoes and lay back for a nap. Golden-green light filtered down through hemlock boughs, and soon he was asleep.

He dreamed of flying. It was a dream he'd had before. He was always walking when it happened, usually along a muddy lane bordered by houses and paddocks. A gust of wind arose, and he simply launched himself up into it. Then he was soaring over the common and the palisade and the salt marsh and the plankings of the wharf and the broad harbor with its small fleet of sailing vessels. Beyond two small wooded islands lay the ocean. Flying over its vast emptiness always made him fearful, and he would steer a banking turn back toward New Meadow. But as he crossed over the palisade, he found himself questioning this newfound ability to fly—when he thought about it, he didn't understand how it could be possible—so to avoid plummeting headlong and shattering his bones, he lowered himself to the ground, landing in a crouch on the close-cropped grass before the Meetinghouse.

As usual, upon waking he felt a terrible sense of loss. The memory of flight remained—the ecstasy of swimming weightless through the air—but the secret of how it was done escaped him as quickly and completely as water sinking into sand.

The day had become overcast. The breeze had started up again, whispering through the canopy and coming down to rattle the beech leaves that clung to the saplings. He really ought to be heading back to the settlement. There was no telling what irritating penances Overlock might be cooking up for him.

He was leaning down to buckle his shoes when the fine hairs at the base of his neck began to prickle. He searched the forest around him, but there was nothing to see: beech trunks, boulders, the fiddleheads of some early ferns. Reaching for the snaphaunce, he started back with a yell of surprise. Cross-legged on a mossy rock not five feet away, with Will's father's musket resting on his lap, sat an Indian. His face was creased like oiled shoe leather, his nose a prominent curved blade. He wore gold hoops in both ears, white doeskin leggings, and a wide-sleeved English huntsman's jacket that had probably been bright scarlet once but had now faded to a pale, salt-stained red.

The savage gazed calmly at Will, who was trembling with shock. It was as if this strange figure had sprouted up fully formed from the moss. Will closed his eyes and kept them shut for a moment. When he opened them, the Indian was still there.

"I didn't hear you coming," Will said. His heart pounded, but he did his best to project a sense of calm. The savage cradled the snaphaunce and observed him steadily. His exact age was impossible to guess, though his braids were silver, and to Will he appeared incalculably ancient. His chest was bare between the faded embroidery on the lapels of the jacket, except for a wampum-bead sash decorated with feathers and a long-sheathed hunting knife.

"Netop," Will said, employing one of the few words he knew in Algonkian. He pointed to his own chest, then to the savage's. "Friend."

The Indian's leathery face was devoid of emotion, the deep-set black eyes as cold and watchful as a hawk's. Will swallowed, glancing at his father's musket resting on the intruder's lap. He gestured toward it. "My piece. May I have it back?"

"Do not be afraid, young sir. I shall not harm you." The man spoke perfect English.

Recovering from his surprise, Will bristled with indignation. He held out his hand, steeling himself to keep it from shaking. "Give me back my musket."

The old Indian, looking amused, handed him the snaphaunce, butt first. Will set it carefully on the rock beside him. "Well now. How is it that you speak such ready English?"

"I mastered your tongue in Old England, Will. The country of your birth."

Will narrowed his eyes. "How do you know my name?"

The old savage gazed back at him. "It is no great feat to discover a young Englishman's name."

"Are you Misquinnipack?" Will asked. "I don't believe I recognize your face from the Saturday market."

"Do you not?" The Indian raised his brows. "But no, Will, I am not *Musqunnipuck.*"

"Well, you'd better not let anyone from New Meadow spot you." Will got to his feet, picking up the musket. "Our Governor has issued a decree against unregistered savages in this valley. If you wish to stay, you must present yourself at the Meetinghouse."

"Unregistered savages? I know little of such matters." The Indian shook his head thoughtfully. "But perhaps it is I who should be asking *you* the questions, Will. Perhaps I should ask, for example, why a young English gentleman feels compelled to venture so far beyond the protective walls of his *palisadoe.*"

Will felt himself blushing. It was true that very few people in New Meadow would be tempted to walk out into the forest alone, even carrying a musket. Fewer still would consider it wise to spend an entire day outside the palisade. But then, he *did* have a reason. "The Governor has put a bounty on a certain black she-wolf. It's been decimating our pastures."

The strange old man nodded. "I see. A hunter." Through a break in the clouds a ray of sunlight came down through the canopy, glinting on the gold hoops in his ears. His braids were fine bright silver, and there were deep creases in the skin around his eyes and mouth. Yet his limbs were long-muscled, and he was lean as a deer. Perhaps he was younger than he'd first appeared to be, Will thought. There was something enviably relaxed, a sort of catlike suppleness, about the way he held himself.

"If you are hunting a she-wolf," he said, "then you're going about it entirely the wrong way. You cannot wait for her to find you, Will. *You* must find *her.*"

"If you know so much about it, why don't *you* slay the wolf? Bring its head to the steps of the New Meadow Meetinghouse, and the Governor will put a gold double crown in your hand. Do you know how many wampum beads you could purchase with such a treasure? How many bolts of rich blue tradecloth?"

The old man stared at him. "I'll take you to her, if you wish."

Will hesitated. He should be hurrying back to the gate, not wandering further into the forest. A handful of bannock was all he'd eaten this morning, and it was nearly suppertime now. The light wouldn't last forever, and he could think of no good reason he should trust this newcomer. Still, if he were to succeed in killing the she-wolf, all sins would be forgiven. He would be a minor hero in New Meadow, and the Poole estate would be two crowns the richer. "Very well," he said. "But if we don't find her soon, I'll need to go back."

They set off further into the wilderness, following no path Will could discern. It was surprisingly hard to keep up with the old Indian. He was at least three inches taller than Will and, though ancient, leapt over boulders and downed trees without breaking his stride. He slipped easily through the same dense briars that caught on Will's clothing and slowed his passage. Again and again Will found himself having to run to keep up, and he would arrive, wide-eyed and panting, to discover the old man resting patiently, his back against a tree or lichen-covered rock.

After a time, the canopy began to open up. The ground became boggy—Will's oxhide shoes were soaked—and a forbidding tangle of willow scrub seemed to block any further progress. Judging from the fetid smell, they were at the edge of a swamp. If Will had been on his own he would have done everything possible to avoid such an area; everyone knew swamps were unwholesome places filled with poisonous creatures and evil vapors. But the savage was striding headlong into the willow scrub. Uneasily, and increasingly light-headed with hunger, Will followed. Alder branches plucked at the sleeves of his doublet, and briars raked stinging scratches across his bare hands and face. Mud sucked at his shoes, and the smell of rotting peat filled his nostrils, though he did his best not to breathe in the vapors.

Emerging from the scrub, they came to water and a kind of natural causeway made up of beaver-downed trees. On either side of these floating logs the swamp was tea-colored but black as it got deeper. Trying to suppress his dismay, Will stepped gingerly across the unstable bridge. The old man had already negotiated it and stood upon a high beaver dam on the other side.

The dam—just a jumble of mud and sticks, but a jumble that offered more solid footing than the causeway—held back a raised pond of glassy water. The Indian waited in silence. The middle of the pond was black, and it was impossible to tell its depth. Along the edges, last summer's leaves lay yellow and perfect under the tea-colored surface. Here and there a log protruded, sun-dried silver and gnawed to a point by an ancestor, perhaps, of the beaver now etching an expanding V across the pond toward its lodge. "So the she-wolf lives *here*?" Will asked.

"Be still." The savage's creased face was inscrutable as he scanned the edges of the swamp. Will rested the heavy butt of the musket on the toe of one shoe, wishing he'd thought to put some corn bannock or even an onion or a piece of dried apple in his doublet pocket. The old man stooped to pull a good-sized stick from the dam. He threw it in a high arc, and it disappeared into a stand of red-twigged dogwood on the far shore of the pond. For a moment, nothing happened. Then a faint rustling came from within the dogwood.

A shadow appeared at the edge of the water. As Will focused his eyes on the shadow, he saw that it was the she-wolf, an immense animal, lean and hungry-looking, with vicious yellow eyes and a pelt that was not pure black but grizzled charcoal. She sniffed the air and looked around but didn't seem to see the two figures on the beaver dam. Three small shadows followed her out of the brush. She had borne whelps, miniature versions of herself with inquisitively raised muzzles and big ears cocked forward. Will primed the musket and raised it to his shoulder. Heart knocking in his chest, he aimed the weapon at a tuft of light fur at the center of the she-wolf's throat. He had no doubt that this was the same predator that had been depleting New Meadow's livestock. The only thing left was to pull the trigger that would spark the flint, but for some reason he couldn't steady his aim. Glancing up, he saw that the old man had placed his hand on the musket barrel and was nudging it lightly back and forth.

"For Heaven's sake, what are you *doing*?" he whispered.

"Are you certain you wish to deprive her pups of their mother, Will? Think of how it was for yourself, losing your mother as a child."

Will lowered the barrel. Ripples of shock radiated outward from his chest. "How do you know about my mother? I'm sure I didn't tell you."

The old Indian ignored him, gazing thoughtfully across the pond at the wary she-wolf. "Go ahead and shoot, Will, if you must. Be quick about it though, for she is beginning to sense something is amiss. Aim well, so that her passing may be swift."

Trying to recover his calm, Will raised the musket and sighted along the barrel at the she-wolf. It was true that he'd lost his mother as a child. She'd been taken by smallpox and buried at sea during the voyage from England nine years ago. He'd been just seven at the time, but he remembered her vividly: kindhearted, articulate, with dancing grey eyes and a musical, trickling laugh that was a source of joy to everyone who heard it. The daughter of a vicar, Sarah Poole had adored Shakespeare. She'd even penned a few of her own plays, giving Will and his older brother, Zeke, the leading roles. The day she'd died was sunny and brisk. The ship's surgeon had stitched her body into sailcloth, a cannonball at her feet. Zeke and Will's father, Thomas Poole, tears streaming down their faces, had heaved her overboard as a single volley was fired from the ship's cannon. Will remembered the sailcloth envelope spiraling downward into clear green depths.

He shook his head to rid himself of the image and tried to focus his concentration on the task at hand. The she-wolf had sensed them. The guard hairs along her spine stood up, and her lips pulled back in a tentative, noiseless snarl.

Will still had a clear shot. He could almost taste the triumph of striding up the Meetinghouse steps with the she-wolf's head held high and the weight and glint of the gold double crown as the Governor placed it in his hand. But for some reason he waited to pull the trigger.

"She's brought about her own death, has she not?" he murmured, squinting down the barrel at the she-wolf. "By murdering our livestock so indiscriminately?"

"Whatever you say, Will." Will lowered the snaphaunce to stare at the Indian. The she-wolf, her gaze alighting on them at last, slipped away into the scrub. Will sighed.

"How is it, exactly, that you discovered my name? And why do you seem to know so much about me?"

The old man gazed at him with a calm intensity. "You have no inkling?"

"No." Will shook his head, unable to decide whether he should be furious, afraid, or simply confused. "I'm quite certain that I've never seen your face before."

The old man nodded, as if a long-held suspicion had been confirmed. "Our paths will cross again, Will. But for the moment, farewell." With that, he leapt down from the beaver dam and set off at a jog across the causeway of floating logs.

"Wait!" Will called, but the old man in the faded huntsman's jacket didn't look back. Will set off after him. His progress across the logs was much slower as he had to look down to ensure his footing, and by the time he reached the other side, the old savage had disappeared. It was as if he'd never been there at all. As if he were a ghost—or a vision.

Two

The old man who called himself Squamiset rested on a cliff above the river, gazing down upon the slow whirl of an eddy. After a time an osprey flew in, circling twice over the eddy and adjusting its powerful wings precisely to come to a perch on the trunk of a birch sapling that slanted out from the cliff. Squamiset raised his head, taking in the wind-ruffled white crown with the horizontal jet-black stripe, the curved black beak, the scornful yellow eye.

"As usual, fish hawk, you have taken your time."

Men are impatient creatures. Even at your age. It is a terrible weakness.

Squamiset gazed down at the eddy. "He does not know me," the old man said after a moment.

And that surprises you?

"I'd assumed he would have had at least a glimmer of it by now."

You assume too much. He does not know he possesses the Sight. What he sees is fractured, and he does not know how to interpret it.

Squamiset sighed. "This isn't going to be easy, is it?"

The osprey eyed him. *Did you ever think it would?*

"I suppose not."

The two beings sat watching sticks and pinecones bob and circle around the eddy before the fast current caught and swept them down the river. After a time, the osprey spread its great wings and leapt from the branch. Squamiset observed it as it flew away, climbing the wind currents in an ascending spiral until it was a tiny black X high in the blue sky, then a pinpoint, then nothing.

Will had lost his way. It was impossible to retrace the path he'd taken with the old Indian because everything in the forest looked different now and yet the same, and it took him hours of blundering about before he could find a well-used trail. By then the light was almost gone, night-fall cloaking the boulders and moss-covered logs in blue shadow. A low rumble of drumbeats spread through the forest like distant thunder. He swore under his breath. Lockout. The Watch giving notice to any strag-glers that the gate was about to be closed for the night.

By the time he came to the edge of the forest, true darkness had set in. There was no moon. A brilliant tapestry of stars reached down to the palisade, which swallowed the bottom of the tapestry in a plane of ink-black shadow. At the gate, he pounded on the thick oak planks. There was no answer at first. He called out for the watchman. A muffled, ill-tempered voice came through the wood.

"Who is it?"

"Will Poole. I was hunting and I got lost. Let me in, please."

"Who?" the watchman on duty asked. "I can't hear your mumbling. Are you a man or a monster?"

Will sighed. He recognized the voice: it was Jack Little, a bachelor who'd done a brief turn as Will's tutor before Will's father had discov-ered that Little had greatly exaggerated the scope of his education. "Will Poole," he repeated loudly.

"Will *Poole*? Why, what are you doing out *there*, boy? I should have thought you'd be in bed by now, resting soundly after an honest day's work. Is there an army of savages out there with you, Will, waiting to pour in through the gate?"

"Must I get down on my knees and beg? Please let me in."

There was a long, savoring silence, then a heavy rattle as the chain was pulled back and, finally, the resonant clink of the iron bolt. Little drew open the gate just enough for Will to step inside, then slammed it shut and bolted it. The watchman turned and fixed Will with a look of smug distaste. "The fine will be expensive, no doubt."

"You *could* forget to report me."

"Ah, but it is my duty to report you, Will. This gate is locked every night for a reason, you know, and I took a grave risk in opening it for you. Would you have me lie on your behalf?"

"I suppose not. Go ahead and report me then."

"Count on it," Little said coldly, grunting with exertion as he strained to draw the massive iron chain through its brackets.

James Overlock sat on a stool by the hearth in the low-ceilinged hall, using a poker to spin a goose on a twisted cord. He'd been working around the house all day, and he was tired of it. Tired of being a servant. Tired of being responsible for a once-prosperous gentleman's estate that now amounted to this modest house, a dwindling supply of gold coins, and one unhappy, rebellious orphan. It wasn't only that young Will's mutinous tendencies had flared to a new level of outrageousness this morning, although that in itself was quite alarming. No, there was something strange about the boy, something uncanny. He was too solitary, for one thing. He had no friends to speak of. More troubling, he seemed to possess a baffling affection for the howling wilderness beyond the palisade, where he spent all too many a day surrounded by who knew what beasts and suspiciously watchful ravens and trees that groaned ominously in the wind. One hated to think about it, but there it was. There were moments when James Overlock feared that his ward might be coming under the influence of Satan.

Will seemed to have no fear of this possibility and was therefore not equipped to resist it. Despite frequent promptings at the Meetinghouse from no less a personage than the Governor himself, and despite daily encouragement from James in the form of regular readings from the Geneva Bible, Will had showed a profound disinterest in receiving God's omnipotent light. It was a dangerous failing—not only for the boy but for anyone associated with him. Particularly for his legal guardian.

The latch on the door clicked open. James shot up, his poor heart stuttering with alarm. But it was only Will, home at last from his wanderings in the eerie forest. James sat back on the stool, examining the boy carefully for signs of spiritual corruption and finding nothing obvious. Will showed every sign of developing into a striking young man, with his father's strong chin and his mother's dark hair and flashing, intelligent eyes. His emotions were always plainly displayed on his face, though he fancied himself secretive; his expression just now was sheepish and guilty.

"You're very tardy," James said severely. Will strode across the hall to the dining table, a single slab that Thomas Poole and Will's elder brother, Zeke, had hewed from a massive white pine they'd felled at the edge of the forest. The table, now beaten and stained from years of use, supported an iron pot covered by a cloth. Will lifted the cloth and peered inside. "May I?"

"Wait for the goose. It's almost done."

"I apologize for being so late," Will said. "I fell asleep, and then I lost the trail."

James nodded, a familiar sensation of suppressed anger constricting his chest. "What is this community supposed to think, Will, of a young man who neglects his chores to spend an entire day and part of a night wandering alone in the demon-infested wilderness?"

Will glanced up sharply. "Why is it your concern what the community thinks?"

James ignored him. "No doubt we shall pay a sizable fine for your tardiness. But honestly, Will, that may be the least of our concerns. Remember, as your legal guardian, I am held to account for your actions."

Will flushed but remained silent.

James spun on his stool and stuck the goose with the poker, causing the fowl's golden-brown skin to hiss and bubble. It was perfectly cooked. "I cannot express the degree to which your behavior pains me, Will. After a lifetime of loyal service to the Poole family, I would expect a little more gratitude from its youngest son—and a good deal more cooperation."

Will bowed his head in a show of contrition. "You have reason to be upset. I'll do my best not to disappoint you in the future."

Taking a deep breath to calm himself, James cut the goose from its cord and placed it on a trencher beside the blackened loblolly pot. He ate in silence. When he was finished, he retreated to his bed, leaving Will alone in the candlelit hall.

Will cut off another succulent portion of gooseflesh with his knife and chewed in silence. Later, he moved to the hearth and sat on the stool before the dying fire. He used the flat-bladed shovel to draw the embers into a pile, placed a split beech log on top, and watched the yellow flames dance up. He was exhausted enough but did not relish the prospect of the cramped sleeping berth.

One by one the candles guttered out, leaving the fire as the only point of light in the hall's low-ceilinged gloom. As a child Will had helped build this house, fetching hammers and holding planks as his father and brother had nailed them in place. There were happy memories here to be sure, but now his father was dead. Zeke was master of a merchant ship. The last time he'd returned to New Meadow was two months ago, early March. He'd asked Overlock to produce the ledger and the small trunk that held the family's gold. Lying awake that night, Will had listened to them murmuring as they checked and re-checked the accounts. At one point, the murmurs had risen to angry accusations. It seemed Overlock had been ordering packages from Liverpool full of silk stockings, linen shirts, and slashed velvet doublets, articles of clothing most people would consider above the station of a household servant. Without consulting Will or Zeke, the steward had also donated a large sum in his own name for repairs to the roof of the New Meadow Meetinghouse. The donation had no doubt been intended to improve Overlock's standing with John E. Rockingham, the well-heeled deacon whom King Charles had appointed First Proprietor and Governor of the New Meadow plantation. The money would make it more likely that Overlock would receive a grant of land once his term of servitude expired the following year, on the occasion of Will's eighteenth birthday.

In the morning, the faces of Will's older brother and Will's legal guardian had been pale and drawn. The Poole fortune, it seemed, was appallingly depleted.

The following day Zeke had set off for the Connecticut River to load a cargo of beaver fur and timber, which he planned to trade for tobacco and molasses in the Barbadoes. Zeke was determined to restore the family's former prosperity, even if that meant spending his entire life at sea. Will, in the meantime, was left alone in the cramped New Meadow cottage with a man he detested—and who clearly detested him.

Three

To keep Overlock happy, Will threw himself into household chores: turning the earth for the herb garden, replacing rotted cedar shingles on the roof, cutting and splitting firewood, making candles of tallow, and helping his guardian butcher a hog. And there were all the tasks that flowed from that gruesome work: grinding and stuffing sausage, brining and hanging bacon and ham, and curing the pigskin for use in shoes and straps. When he was not working, Will was slaving over figures and memorizing passages from the Geneva Bible or attending services at the close-packed Meetinghouse, sitting on a hard pew as the word of God shook the very air around him.

On occasion he did manage to steal away. One spring morning, hungering for a long view of the sea, he climbed the ridge known as East Rock and sat looking out over the greening forest at the sparkling blue ocean beyond. The sun on his face felt good. From the pocket of his doublet he took his whittling knife and a piece of basswood he'd been carving into a toy *mishoon*, the dugout canoe the local savages used to ply the rivers and bays. When the vessel was done, he planned to whittle three tiny figures kneeling in its hull. He thought he might give it to one of the children at the Misquinnipack village—although Governor Rockingham had forbidden English visitation there, so Will wouldn't be able to deliver the toy himself. But he thought perhaps he could give it to one of the half-dozen savages the Governor permitted to trade furs and shellfish at the Saturday market on the common.

The project took him back to his own childhood, soon after he and his brother and father—recently bereft and widowed by the death of Sarah Poole—had first arrived in America. They'd been building the plantation in those days, felling trees to construct the palisade, the Meetinghouse, the mill, and bridges and wharves and cottages. Will had been too young for that sort of work, and his father, not knowing what else to do with him, had allowed him to play on the riverbank with the Misquinnipack children. This was before Governor Rockingham had written the order forbidding contact with the local savages. Will remembered catching trout with lines made from braided bark and hooks carved from bone. He remembered learning to steer a *mishoon* just like the miniature one he was now whittling and stealing off into the forest to discover swimming holes. He remembered a ravine where cold water tumbled over sun-warmed granite to create waterslides and effervescing natural bathtubs, filtered sunlight playing on boulders and moss, and daring Misquinnipack boys diving from high rocks into crystalline pools of water. They'd had a name for Will back then: Toyusk. He'd asked, and they'd shown him with signs and gestures that it meant "ford" or "crossing," a name that still puzzled him. Last summer he'd gone back to look for the ravine with the natural bathtubs and waterslides, but he hadn't been able to find it on his own.

Feeling sleepy, he put the knife away and rested his back against a boulder. He'd almost drifted off when he sensed a presence and opened his eyes. On the reddish stone beside him, craggy head supported comfortably on a pillow of grass, lay the elderly savage who'd brought him to the she-wolf. Will nodded, pretending not to be surprised. "I was wondering if I would see you," he began, but the old man held up his hand. His eyes were closed, and he appeared deep in thought, the great hooked nose pointing straight up at the sky.

"Tell me, Will," he asked after a moment. "Have you ever conversed with a Manitoo?"

Will thought. "I suppose a Manitoo is one of your demons?"

The savage looked disappointed, as if Will were a promising student who'd failed some easy test. "Come," he said, springing to his feet. "Let us hunt."

Will took the musket and followed him along the trail that led down from the ridge. After a few moments the old savage froze, cocking his head as if to listen. Will just managed to stop without running into him. At first he heard nothing. Then he noticed a kind of low clucking purr, and a flock of turkeys—ugly birds strutting briskly with their warty, featherless heads craned forward—began to cross the trail ten yards ahead. Will raised the musket to his shoulder, aimed, and pulled the trigger. The flint sparked, the pan sizzled, and the birds panicked, flapping up into the air. With a wonderful deftness the old man nocked and loosed an arrow. One of the turkeys stopped mid-flight and plummeted to the ground—the arrow threaded neatly through its middle—as the loud echo of Will's musket report dissipated in the trees.

"Good shot," Will remarked.

"A bow is stealthier than a musket," the savage said, kneeling over the fallen turkey. He rested his hand on the bird's wattled neck as if to comfort it. "The bow man can shoot quickly, one arrow after the other, while the musket man must pause to recharge his powder." With a smooth decisive stroke, he withdrew the bloodied arrow, wiped it on the leaf litter, and slid it back into its rolled-bark quiver. "An arrow, unlike a ball, can be used again." Will nodded, absorbing the lesson.

The next afternoon the old man, who said his name was Squamiset, told Will to find a tall tree and climb it. "Just stay there," he instructed, "and observe what passes on the ground."

Will found a great oak with its first branches low enough that he could hoist himself up. He left the musket leaning against the trunk and climbed. After half an hour, he became restless. Overlock had been pleased to receive yesterday's turkey, but even so, it had not been easy for Will to steal away again. He wanted to make the most of his time in the forest, and that did not involve sitting uselessly on a tree branch. He was readying himself to climb down when he spied a huge black bear ambling toward him across the leaf litter.

He froze, never having seen a bear this close. He knew what the beasts could do, though: several months earlier, with a few swipes of its claws, one had killed two mastiffs belonging to Captain Hooker, the leader of the Governor's militia. This bear, a large one in Will's estimation, came to a stop at the base of the oak. It grunted and peered hungrily up into the branches. Will held his breath.

The bear sniffed the breeze. It rose on its hind legs, placing its amply clawed forepaws on the oak trunk. It opened its mouth to reveal a scarlet tongue and huge yellow teeth and let out a bellow that shook the air. Little jolts of fear shot through Will's limbs. He couldn't climb down. The bear would easily catch him, even if he somehow managed to evade it at the base of the tree. So he climbed further up, high into the oak's uppermost branches. The bear roared, raking its claws on the trunk. Will's musket toppled into the leaf litter. He cursed himself for not bringing it with him.

Suddenly he noticed Squamiset below him in the tree, seated comfortably on a curving branch. "How long have *you* been up here?"

"I see that you have attracted the interest of a bear," the old Indian observed drily.

Will stared down at it. The bear pawed at the lowest branch, as if considering whether it was worth its while to climb.

"What if it decides to come up after us?"

The old man shrugged. "In that case, we are finished."

Will felt a dropping in his stomach. "Can we throw sticks at it to get it to go away and leave us alone?"

"We could. But this is a young male, eager to assert his territory. Such gestures would not be likely to frighten him."

"Can you shoot it with your bow, then?"

"That would be unwise. Bears can withstand even the best-aimed arrows. It would just make him angrier."

Will stared down at the massive predator. It sent up another horrifying bellow, as if infuriated that Will would dare to meet its gaze. "Well, what should we do?"

"Wait."

So they waited. The bear stayed where it was, roaring up at them occasionally, but it didn't climb the tree. After a time it seemed to become bored. Then, to Will's immeasurable relief, it ambled away into the forest.

"How is it that you always know exactly where I am?" he asked as they climbed down from the tree. "And how do you manage to appear and disappear without me seeing you?"

Squamiset looked amused. "It's no great trick to discover an Englishman in the forest, Will. And it's easy for a person to believe he is alone in a tree when in fact he is not. Do you understand?"

Will bent to retrieve his musket from the leaf litter. "I suppose so." But the truth was, he remained puzzled.

April blossomed into May. The forest filled with the scent of blooming trees and the endless choruses of songbirds. Squamiset gave Will a bow carved of walnut and strung with moose sinew and a rolled-bark quiver of arrows fletched with turkey feathers. Will was a quick learner and reasonably coordinated, but he despaired of ever being as deft as Squamiset, who could pluck a bounding squirrel from a branch with hardly a sideways look.

If it were Will's decision alone, he would have spent all his waking moments in the forest. The house felt more restrictive every time he went back, as did the entire plantation. Sometimes within the palisade he found himself struggling to breathe, as if he were actually running out of air.

In addition to Overlock's unending chores and his daily readings from the Geneva Bible, Will was required to spend the better part of two days a week on a hard bench at the Meetinghouse. Sunday was Divine Service, and Thursday was Lessons. Everyone over the age of fourteen had to attend both functions. There were volunteer ushers who wandered the aisles with long feather-tipped sticks; when someone began to doze, they would reach over and tickle him awake. Will kept them busy. The ushers watched him constantly with disapproving frowns.

Governor Rockingham was, among other things, an ordained deacon who spoke from the pulpit with fiery conviction. As a young man he'd been a military adventurer. He was said to have served as a mercenary with the Protestant forces in Bohemia and later as a lieutenant with Sir Walter Raleigh on his 1616 expedition to search for El Dorado. On occasion, as when he appeared to help Captain Hooker drill New Meadow's volunteer militia, he could still be seen wearing his steel corselet and boat-brimmed helmet. But his interest in soldiering amounted to nothing compared to his religious passion. The Governor was known throughout New England as a man of exemplary piety, and he was a thunderously effective preacher. Indeed, looking around the Meetinghouse, Will could see that his words held most of the New Meadow population rapt.

For his own part, Will constantly felt like an impostor. In certain moments Rockingham's pale blue eyes settled squarely upon him, examining Will coolly as he preached. It was as if the Governor-deacon could see into Will's soul—as if he were storing away what he found there for future use.

Mostly, though, Will's mind wandered. Sometimes it was the hallucinations. He would find himself plummeting through a layer of fluffy clouds or sitting in the prow of a boat on a boundless steel-grey ocean or looking down from the ceiling of the village tavern. Then he would open his eyes and find himself back in the pew, pretending to absorb the teachings of New Meadow's most distinguished preacher. In such moments Will felt a frantic despair rising within him. Perhaps he was losing his mind. Or perhaps it was worse: perhaps he truly was possessed. Maybe these flashing visions were Satan's way of poisoning his feelings about Christianity and encouraging him to pursue the path of sin. If so, it was a good strategy on the Devil's part. More and more as the weeks ground on, Will came to dread the hour when he would have to trudge beside Overlock across the grassy common to the Meetinghouse.

Squamiset had the ability to stay motionless for hours. He thought nothing of spending an entire morning chin-deep in a lily pond. He prepared ingenious traps with whiplike saplings and cords of twisted bark. He was a wise and patient teacher, always willing to share his hunting secrets. And yet Will found some of the old man's ways disconcerting.

One breezy afternoon, for example, they were resting beside the Misquinnipack River. Bankside oak branches groaned and knocked in the wind, which licked shifting patterns on the surface of the slow-moving current. Squamiset had seemed distracted all day, inattentive and unusually quiet, as if some grave matter weighed on his mind. Now on the grassy riverbank he was flat on his back, napping with his arms crossed over his chest. His jaw had fallen open, and his light snores blended with the murmur of the river and the whistling of the wind in the trees.

Will took the opportunity to peer at the Indian's unusual face: the great bladelike nose, the tracery of scars and wrinkles covering the leathered brown cheeks, the gold hoop earrings, the bright silver braids. He quite liked this old man who had so much to teach and did so with dry wit and a pleasant, affable manner. But then a strange thing happened. As Will watched in consternation, a hairy black bumblebee the size of a man's thumb joint emerged from Squamiset's gaping mouth and crawled onto his lip. It paused a moment, as if getting its bearings, then buzzed off into the gusting breeze.

"Squamiset!" Will cried out in alarm. "You'd better wake up." He shook the old man's shoulder, but there was no response. His cheeks were warm to the touch, and he was snoring, but otherwise it was as if he were dead. Will shook him harder. Then he got to his feet and edged away in panic. What could it mean when bees hived inside a man's sleeping body? It couldn't be a good thing. It might be a demonic thing.

Will came back and knelt beside the sleeping Indian. Perhaps he'd imagined it. Perhaps the bee had only *landed* on Squamiset's face and not come crawling out of his mouth, as it had seemed.

Then Will heard a loud drone, and the bee zigzagged in and buzzed around his head before alighting on the old man's chin. Will tried to brush it off with the sleeve of his doublet, but after buzzing and circling angrily, the bee landed again. Will watched, incredulous, as the huge insect crawled over Squamiset's lip and disappeared into his open mouth. A moment later, the old man sat up. He looked thoughtful and well rested. Will stared at him, torn between relief and horror. "Answer me truthfully," he said. "Are you in league with Satan or not?"

The old man looked amused. "Satan holds little sway on this continent, Will, despite what you may hear in your Meetinghouse."

"Well then, you are a sorcerer."

The old man got up, stretched his arms, and crouched at the edge of the river. He cupped his hands in the clear water and brought some up to his lips. "I am a *powwaw*. There is no translation for this word. A *powwaw* is not a sorcerer. With the help of the Manitoo, my spirit can travel outside my body, as you have seen. In this way I can be in two places at once, and in visions and dreams I may catch fleeting glimpses of the future or the past. Also, I can occasionally create believable illusions in the minds of others. These are my only powers. None of it is what I would call sorcery." He dried his hands on his tunic and turned, his eyes meeting Will's with sudden intensity. "But here's a question for you, Will. Are you aware that you possess similar abilities?"

Will let that sink in. "That's impossible. I'm not even an Indian." But even as he denied it, a part of him knew that it could be true. The hallucinations. Perhaps they weren't symptoms of approaching madness after all, or indications of Satanic possession. Perhaps they were just signs of some untapped natural skill. It was a wonderfully encouraging idea.

Squamiset came to sit beside him on the bank. His timeworn face was solemn. "Many people possess these talents, Will, but most never know it, and fewer still learn how to master them. It takes a great deal of time and effort."

"Is one required to invite bumblebees into his mouth?"

Squamiset suppressed a smile. "One finds his own path. To gain true mastery, it is necessary to enlist the aid of the Manitoo."

"I'm not sure about these Manitoo, Squamiset. That is, you've mentioned them before. You speak of them as friends or helpers. My people would call them demons, but regardless of where they come from, isn't it dangerous to call upon such beings?"

The old man reached down for his bow and quiver and got to his feet. "The Manitoo come in many guises, Will. In time, I hope, you will meet one yourself. Then you can decide whether they are friends or demons."

Will never shared this conversation with Overlock, of course, nor with anyone else in the plantation. To do so would have been extremely foolish. People had been whipped, pilloried, branded, and publicly shamed for less—for seemingly minor offenses such as not attending Divine Service for two consecutive weeks, using the Lord's name in vain, or kissing the hand of a married woman in the street. Three months ago, a carpenter named Caleb June had had his ear sliced off for the crime of harboring a Baptist in his home. The Baptist was June's wife's cousin, newly arrived from Northamptonshire. Will could only imagine how Governor Rockingham would react if he learned about Will's conversation with Squamiset on the riverbank. He would consider it heresy, plain and simple.

It was a good thing Will himself wasn't a devout Puritan, or his interactions with Squamiset would have filled him with fear for the health of his immortal soul. As it was, he was content to keep the friendship secret. If, in the course of becoming a better hunter, he was accidentally exposed to a bit of harmless witchery, so be it. He was willing to take the risk.

A diligent student, Will's competence increased. He brought back a regular supply of game for Overlock: rabbit, turkey, waterfowl, and a small white-tail buck, which he dressed in the forest, with Squamiset's help, and carried back to New Meadow on his shoulders. To avoid the suspicion his carved Indian bow and the quiver of arrows might stir, it was his habit to leave them hidden in a hollow tree near the edge of the forest. On his way out he would stow the snaphaunce, shot wallet, and powder horn in the tree, and before presenting himself at the gate he would retrieve them. He skinned the game and cured the hides in the lean-to attached to the parlor. He made sure, as Squamiset directed, to express his gratitude to the spirits of the beings that had given their lives for his sustenance.

Overlock was grudgingly pleased to receive the extra meat, and for a time he didn't question Will's improving fortunes as a hunter. Not, that is, until a fresh May evening over a rabbit stew spiced luxuriously with expensive East India pepper. They were dining by the light of three guttering candles when Overlock broke the silence that was the norm between them. "Where have you been hunting exactly, Will?"

Will was ready for this. "On the ridges, mainly, and in the swamps."

The steward made a sour face. "You really ought to steer clear of swamps, which are breeding grounds for all manner of evil. Terrible diseases, poisons of the blood, demonic airs, and suchlike."

Will swabbed his trencher with a piece of corn bread. "I used to believe that too. But the truth is, they're not so bad. And game animals do like to shelter in them."

Overlock gazed at him with polite amazement. "It's strange, now that I think about it. I never hear the reports of your musket."

Suddenly alert, Will straightened in his chair. "I've found that noises do not carry far in the forest."

Overlock looked unconvinced. In the end, though, Will wasn't too worried. If his guardian were more observant, he would have noticed that the holes in the hides now curing in the lean-to hadn't been made by musket balls. Overlock had his own concerns.

They chewed in silence. Overlock's plump cheeks shone in the candlelight, and the pointed King Charles beard glistened with fat. After a time, he put down his knife and cleared his throat. "I do hope you're being cautious, Will. This afternoon in the tavern, we heard reports of a dangerous intruder."

Will covered his surprise by lifting his tankard for a swallow of Overlock's excellent home-brewed beer. "An intruder?"

The steward nodded, his small deep-set eyes intent on Will's face. "Old Judas was spotted in the Misquinnipack village."

"Old Judas?"

Overlock nodded. "Apparently this primitive spent a decade in London as a domestic servant in some nobleman's household. He betrayed his benefactor by tricking him into outfitting a ship for New England, where he immediately slipped back into the forest. Hence the name Judas. He is said to be a tall and elderly savage with excellent English and a deceptively handsome bearing. One of their sorcerers, apparently. A notorious traitor and an irredeemable slave to Satan."

Will avoided his guardian's eyes by ladling another serving of stew onto his trencher, though his appetite had suddenly vanished. "A sorcerer, you say."

"Yes. One of their witch doctors. It's said that he can summon a living snake from a sloughed-off skin. That he can produce a green leaf in winter by burning a dead one and crumbling the ashes into water. That he can walk ankle-deep in granite, shrink himself to the size of an ant, or sail across a lake in a mussel shell. Minor conjuring tricks, you understand, which he is granted in exchange for his allegiance to Satan, whom the savages call *Hobbamock*."

Will nodded, feigning a deep interest in his plate of stew. Before meeting Squamiset, he never would have believed such tales. But now— well, he didn't think Squamiset was a Devil-worshipper. According to the old man, Hobbamock was no more than an especially powerful Manitoo, one of many, like Weewillmac, the horned water snake, or Yotaanit, the Fire Bringer. Of course Will couldn't risk explaining this to Overlock. But there was little doubt in his mind that "Old Judas" and Squamiset were the same person.

Four

Squamiset possessed the Sight. Sometimes, as with the bumblebee, he used it to travel outside his body, to see what was happening at the present moment in places other than where his physical being rested. Other times, the Sight came to him in visions. Squamiset did not make the visions—they were made by something greater—but he had learned how to control them and how to linger and move within them. He remained attentive to every detail, because the visions had a meaning that extended far beyond himself.

Often past and future could be hard to distinguish, but today there was no mistaking the past, because it was his own story, and it was etched in his mind like scars in flesh. A summer village on the seashore, sheltered by high dunes. Long days spent gathering food—spearing fish and lobster in clear saltwater and digging for clams in the tide-moistened sand. Ball games on a flat beach, nights feasting by firelight. A beautiful young woman, his wife, her smooth oval face blurred and shifting as if he were seeing her from beneath the washing pond as she gazed down at her own reflection those many seasons ago.

The English arrived in the year of their God 1602. The ship was like a new kind of cloud, crisp on the horizon as it materialized upon the sea. Some refused to see it, calling it an illusion, a trick of light on water. Others, overcome with dread, ran away into the forest. A group of young men, Squamiset among them, painted their faces and paddled out to meet the ship, chanting as they crossed the water so that the sound of their own voices would give them courage. The Englishmen were pale and wild-looking, crowding the decks in broad-brimmed hats and finery, with beards like bull elk. Their tongue was foreign to Squamiset then, guttural gibberish like the language of dogs or seals. They called down to the *mishoons*, enticing the young men with silver chalices and bolts of vivid blue cloth that snapped in the wind.

The vision world receded. Squamiset sighed, opening his eyes. He was alone, sitting cross-legged on a bearskin by the firepit in the home of his host, the Musqunnipuck sachim. His long clay pipe had gone out, so he used his knife to pry down into the white cinders for a live ember. Inhaling deeply, he breathed in a great cloud of pokeweed smoke and the vision world rushed back into his mind.

He was paddling over the ocean with the English boy, Will Poole. The sea was storm-tossed, high waves building and crashing all around them. This was no longer the realm of memory. This was an altogether less predictable and more frightening place: the realm of what was to come.

The boy was ashen-faced and wide-eyed, gripping his paddle in terror. The sky was a bruised purple, and a gusting wind enveloped them so that it was a struggle to keep the *mishoon* from getting swamped. The waves were immense, as big as English houses. They lifted the small boat upward for a queasy long view—sea foam scudding along the surface in an endless field of white-capped chaos—then plunged them down into the chasm between the swells, where they were walled in on all sides by opaque green seawater. The *mishoon* rose up on the waves and plunged down. Again and again the waves threatened to swallow them, but somehow the *mishoon* always righted itself.

Time seemed to accelerate. Clouds rushed across the sky, massing and breaking up, and then were swept away altogether, leaving the sky blue and the day windless. A brilliant sun beat down upon his bare shoulders, and the air was fragrant and moist. In the prow of the *mishoon*, the boy had dozed off. The water was calm now, glassy green over a shallow bottom of white sand and dark eelgrass. Fish the length of Squamiset's forearm cruised the bottom in groups of three and four, fast green shadows zigzagging across the sand like restless ghosts. Beyond the prow of the *mishoon* the bottom deepened to a channel of midnight blue, and beyond that was a pure white beach backed by a wind-battered fringe of vegetation. An island. Was this Sowwaniu, home of the Bringer of Seeds?

The vision world melted away. Squamiset found himself back in the Musqunnipuck sachim's longhouse, and there was a commotion outside. Guttural English voices shouted over the baying of dogs. The voices were angry and demanding. Softer voices responded, Musqunnipuck voices, confused and increasingly upset. And then the Englishmen were saying his name—not his true name but the nickname he'd been given upon his escape from captivity—Old Judas.

He got to his feet and ducked through the sealskin door flap and into the bright sunshine. Seven English militiamen faced the assembled Musqunnipuck in the central courtyard of the village. The English wore brass corselets strapped across their chests. They had boat-shaped helmets and cutlasses stuck in their belts. One carried a trumpet-barreled gun, a blunderbuss, and three others held pikes, long spearlike weapons with sharpened steel blades that glinted menacingly in the sun. A fifth man held the leashes of three huge mastiffs that growled balefully at the Musqunnipuck dog pack, which had gathered round to bare their teeth from a safe distance.

When Squamiset emerged, the leader of the soldiers turned to stare at him. He was a ruddy Englishman of late middle age with a graying copper beard and cruel grey eyes shaded by his boat-brimmed helmet. This man gave an order and held up a freckled, callused hand. The Englishman controlling the mastiffs jerked the cords, and the dogs whimpered into silence. "You are Old Judas?" the captain asked.

"It is not my true name," Squamiset replied in English, "but you are free to call me by it." His eyes ached from the bright sun, but he could see that the entire Musqunnipuck band had been drawn by the disturbance. Some of their faces, particularly those of the younger men, were hard with anger. Others were pale and full of fear. This was not an auspicious turn of events. The Musqunnipuck village was but a few leagues from New Meadow. To have armed Englishmen standing within the palisade of one's own village was like glimpsing the shadow of doom.

The copper-bearded captain cleared his throat. He was older than he looked, perhaps, beneath the faded whiskers. "You are to leave this valley at once or face death."

"I've done nothing wrong," Squamiset protested calmly. "I am simply visiting friends."

"Your very presence is wrong. It violates our laws, as established by the Providence of our omnipotent Lord and as administered by his Excellency, John E. Rockingham. You are to leave at once."

"A man is not free to go where he pleases, then, even in his own country?"

The militia captain's tight smile revealed a row of blunt white teeth. "It's not your country anymore, Judas. Now I shall repeat this order once, and only once. You are to leave here of your own accord. If you are spotted in this vicinity again, you shall be arrested and put to death. Do you understand?"

Squamiset gazed back impassively. For many years he'd kept his distance from all English settlements, and events such as this reminded him why. Yet now was not the time for angry words. Resistance would only create more trouble for his hosts. He bowed his head. "I will go. Give me a moment to take leave of my friends."

The grey-eyed captain shot a glance at the man holding the dogs. "No moment, Judas. You are to leave right now. These men will escort you. I counsel you: do not resist."

Squamiset shook his head ruefully and murmured a few words in Algonkian. There was a movement in the crowd, and this sparked a series of reactions. The pikemen dropped to crouching positions, slashing their weapons down to point at the center of Squamiset's chest. The Englishman with the blunderbuss swept the gaping barrel back and forth across the murmuring crowd. "H*old!*" Squamiset shouted in English, raising both his hands. "I have only asked this woman to retrieve my belongings."

The Musqunnipuck sachim's third wife, her pretty face pinched with fear, backed up to the longhouse and slipped in through the entry flap. The militia captain made a circling gesture with one stubby, freckled finger, and the pikemen posted their weapons and stepped forward to take Squamiset's arms. For just an instant he succumbed to his anger and threw off their grasp with an ease that must have surprised them. They tried to take his arms again, but this time a band of young Musqunnipucks stepped forward to prevent them, forming a protective circle around their honored guest. "Desist, my friends," Squamiset said in Algonkian, and the youths reluctantly blended back into the crowd.

In the confusion, however, one of the young Musqunnipucks had caught the copper-bearded captain around the neck, and he was now pressing a sharp hunting knife to the man's hairy throat. Squamiset's stomach dropped. The boy was Natoncks, the son of the sachim's third wife. He would not be forgiven for embarrassing the English captain in this way.

With their leader held hostage, the other Englishmen found themselves on the edge of panic. They wheeled around, swinging their weapons dangerously from one potential assailant to the next. The mastiffs howled, provoking an answering chorus from the Musqunnipuck dogs.

"Let him go," Squamiset said, silently chiding himself for having chosen to stay within the village and not on his own in the forest. The Sight was neither infallible nor comprehensive. He could not choose which aspects of the future it showed him. Still, he might have foreseen an event like this.

"No, grandfather." The brash young Musqunnipuck shook his head. He pressed the knife harder against the Englishman's throat as the latter twitched, his red-bearded jaws clenched in fury. "These coat-men have dishonored you enough, and I can see through this one's washed-out eyes into his soul. He deserves to die."

At that moment the sachim's third wife emerged from the long-house with Squamiset's bow, quiver, and hastily packed bundle of belongings. When she saw her son holding his red-bearded hostage, she let out a soft cry of anguish. She understood what Squamiset under-stood: this could not end well.

"Let him go," Squamiset repeated in Algonkian. After a moment, Natoncks released the Englishman with a shove, and the man pitched forward into the dust. He lay there for a moment, then got to his feet. He bent to pick up his steel helmet, dusted it off, and put it back on his head. His freckled face was as red as a steamed lobster.

"Arrest this criminal," he ordered in a hoarse voice, his furious grey eyes darting a glance at Natoncks as he rubbed his throat above its broad linen collar. The soldiers surrounded the boy, twisting his arms behind his body. Natoncks' mother covered her mouth with her hand. Squamiset placed his hand on her shoulder. Her son was now a prisoner of the New Meadow militia. The soldiers were too heavily armed; if any of the Musqunnipuck tried to resist, there would be a massacre. "Escort the witch doctor to the northbound trail," the red-faced captain ordered. "Make sure you observe him as he goes. If he so much as looks back over his shoulder, cut him down. The young criminal comes with me."

Squamiset took his belongings from Natoncks' stricken mother as the soldiers bound the boy's wrists and led him away, shoving him forward and pricking his back with the blades of their pikes. Thankfully, the boy knew enough to understand that further resistance would only lead to his death.

The soldiers assigned to escort Squamiset out of the valley took his arms gingerly, and this time he didn't throw them off. There was no point in it. He would go in peace.

Five

Will spent the morning squelching through shin-deep mud in the salt marshes east of town, hunting geese with the snaphaunce instead of the bow and arrow. The salt marshes were not the forest, he reasoned, and his being there would not provoke as much suspicion. The afternoon was mild and sunny, warm for mid-May, with the fragrance of cherry blossoms in the air. But there was a foreboding mood about the day that Will couldn't quite fathom. He would have expected birdsong, for example, or a breeze ruffling the salt grass, but an eerie silence prevailed over the broad marshes and the forest's edge. It was as if the whole valley were holding its breath.

He had to warn Squamiset that the Governor's men would be on the lookout. Unfortunately, though Will had given him every opportunity, Squamiset had not appeared today. There was no sign of the old man. Will had become worried.

With a fat goose in one hand and the musket in the other, he was crossing the bridge over the millstream when he was surprised to find Overlock leaning against a boulder in the shade of a spreading elm. The steward's head was bent to the task of whittling a basswood rattle. Whittling was a hobby the two of them shared—as Will saw it, one of the few things they had in common apart from their long history together. The little rattles Overlock made were ingenious, each forming a kind of cage containing a sphere that could be jangled around within its wooden confines. The steward had taken to giving them out as birthday presents to the plantation's children, which gave him an extra dash of popularity, like an eccentric but conscientious uncle.

Will didn't like the self-satisfied look on Overlock's apple-cheeked face this afternoon, and he didn't like that the steward had traded his workaday leather apron for one of the expensive outfits he'd ordered from Liverpool: mouse-colored silken breeches, fine black stockings, and an embroidered serge doublet with falling lace at the cuffs and collar. Will's scalp prickled. Something was afoot.

He strode up to the whittling steward. Overlock, finishing a particularly absorbing piece of knife-work, glanced up, bright-eyed and cheerful. "Hurry home, Will. Governor Rockingham will visit us the moment I send word."

Will's stomach churned. "What's the occasion?"

"Trouble with the savages. He wishes to question you."

"I've done nothing wrong."

"If you are guilty of no sin, Will, then indeed you have nothing to fear. Clean yourself up. I'll delay long enough for you to change your clothing."

Will hurried in through the gate, past garden beds and neatly fenced corrals, across the common with its cockeyed Meetinghouse (the oldest public building in the colony, it had been shoddily constructed and was beginning to buckle under the weight of its slate roof), and past the small brick tavern at the common's edge, which had once been the favorite haunt of his father and remained Overlock's preferred spot to hear the latest gossip. A few acquaintances called out from gardens and rooftops, but Will was so nervous that he could barely return their greetings.

He turned down the narrow lane to his house, which his father, with an eye to the shipping trade, had situated at the gap where the palisade met the harbor. Beyond the house was a spit of land with a meandering creek emptying into a narrow salt marsh. A walkway Will and his brother, Zeke, had built of stout hemlock pilings and planks of Atlantic cedar spanned the salt marsh, connecting the walled village to the wharf and the harbor. Will glanced longingly at the small fleet of sloops and pinnaces riding the wavelets in the cold green water. Against all reason he looked for the trim outlines of Zeke's Bermuda-rigged schooner, but there was to be no such stroke of luck today. Zeke was in the Sugar Islands or the Barbadoes by now. He wouldn't be coming back to New Meadow for months.

Will hung the goose on a hook in the lean-to and splashed water from the basin onto his face. He climbed the ladder to his low-roofed sleeping berth and changed into his best clothes: black breeches and stockings, a green baize doublet with red tape at the sleeves, and a collar of Guilford linen. Down in the parlor, he lit a few candles and sat fidgeting at the slab table. As befitted a house that had never known a female mistress, the furnishings were adequate but Spartan: the slab table, two rough benches, three stools, two fine imported Windsor chairs, and a handsome oak sea chest his father had hauled across the Atlantic nine years before. Overlock's little cage rattles decorated all the windowsills, and the nubs of innumerable candles congregated at the center of the table. Will had never given the tabletop a second thought before, but now, with Governor Rockingham coming, it struck him as slovenly, and he set about picking at the wax drippings with his fingernails.

Hearing voices outside, he got to his feet. The latch clicked, the door creaked open, and in came Overlock with His Excellency the Governor. Will put one foot forward and bowed deeply, as was the custom among English gentlemen. Rockingham returned the gesture in a perfunctory way, touching the crown of his plumed cavalier hat. For the zealous Puritan Will knew the Governor to be, he was remarkably grand, with velvet breeches, silk hose, an embroidered black doublet with slashed sleeves showing some rich scarlet fabric, and a broad, starched ruff of lace at the neck. He cultivated a silver V-shaped beard and a broad, stiffly waxed mustache that reminded Will of portraits he'd seen of the Governor's former associate, Sir Walter Raleigh.

Overlock minced shamelessly, hurrying to arrange the spindle-backed chairs in the center of the room, one facing the other. Will's heart pounded. From the placement of the chairs, it was clear this was not just a friendly visit. It was an interrogation.

Rockingham, smiling at Will, gestured to one of the chairs. He placed his hat on the floor and sat in a chair while Overlock hovered submissively in his orbit, shifting from foot to foot and fussing with the hooks of his new doublet. Will's eyes were drawn to the Governor's hat, the plume and brim of which were a deep, inky black. It looked ominous to Will in the dim light, like a gaping hole in the floor.

"Let me go straight to the point," the Governor began. "It is said, Will, that you've struck up a kind of secret apprenticeship with Old Judas, a Wampanoag savage known to be transient in this valley. Is that so?"

Although he'd been more than half expecting it, Will's heart froze. Rockingham's pale blue eyes seemed to have the power to read his thoughts, and Will struggled to clear his mind of anything that might be construed as heresy. "I'm not familiar with any Indian answering to that name, Your Excellency."

"Come now, Will. The savage is also known as Spanish John. And, in his own tongue, I believe, Squamiset. Do I jog your memory?"

Will colored deeply. There was no longer any possibility of hiding the truth. He would have to spill everything and hope that Squamiset had had the instinct to flee. "He was teaching me the Indian way of hunting, Your Excellency. There was no harm in it."

"Is that so?" Rockingham's gaze was unrelenting. Unable to withstand it, Will stared at the floor. "How did you come to meet this savage, Will? Did you seek him out?"

"No, sir. I happened upon him one morning while I was hunting the she-wolf. I wanted the bounty you'd posted, sir."

"Well, now. And did you encounter the she-wolf?"

Will hesitated. "Yes, sir."

"Did you attempt to shoot it?"

Will fidgeted in the high-backed chair. "Not exactly, sir."

Rockingham raised his brows. "Why ever not? You'd been stalking it with the intention of collecting my bounty, yes?"

"Yes, sir. But it had whelps."

Rockingham glanced up at Overlock, who stood with his hands clasped behind his back, his face carefully neutral. "All the more reason to kill it, Will, I should think. No?"

Will shrugged, his cheeks on fire. He had nothing to say.

"You are a strange and solitary young man," the Governor remarked. "Do you agree?"

"I suppose—well, yes, sir, I suppose I *do* agree." Outside, the sun was sinking low. Part of the palisade was visible through a diamond-paned window, the rough bark on the closely heeled logs lit with a rich orange light. From the harbor came the faint, high-pitched screams of seagulls. Will wished he could stroll down to the dock and sit on the edge of the harbor as he used to do when he was a child, staring out at the water as his innocent thoughts wandered. He wished his father were alive, or that Zeke's sloop had returned and was anchored in the harbor. He wished many things. Above all, he wished to be anywhere else but here.

The Governor's voice now took on a softer tone. "Are you aware, Will, that your Squamiset is a conjurer?"

Will had a sudden coughing fit, and tears came into his eyes. He was finding it very hard to breathe, as if the three of them had used up the limited supply of air in the house. He risked a glance at Overlock, pleading silently for his guardian to open the door and let in the afternoon breeze, but the steward was riveted, immovable.

"You do understand, I take it, that a savage conjurer is what he is because he has made a covenant with Satan?"

Will glanced up for an instant, then swallowed and lowered his gaze.

Rockingham's voice was cold. "Do you concur with what I just said, Will, or not? Answer the question, if you please."

After a long, awkward moment, Will sighed and looked up. "Yes, sir. I concur."

"Good. Good." Rockingham paused, gave Overlock a wry glance, and used one long-fingered hand to pantomime the action of drinking. Overlock sprang to it, nearly tripping on his shoes as he hurried off. A moment later he came back with a foaming tankard of homemade beer. Rockingham reached for the mug, took a long swallow, and wiped his elegant silver mustache on the cuff of his sleeve. He put the tankard down on the floor beside the ominous black hat.

"Just a few more questions, Will, and then we shall be finished for the day. Know that your honesty in these matters, along with your father's laudable service to the New Meadow enterprise, will help tip the scales of justice in your favor. Has Old Judas mentioned the names of any savages that might be conspiring against us? Wambusco, for example, or the Narragansett rabble-rouser Canonicus? Or the mischievous savage known as Old Aesop?

Will worked up the nerve to meet those icy blue eyes. "He mentioned none of those names, sir. He was teaching me the Indian way of hunting, nothing more."

"How about *Natoncks*?"

"Natoncks?" Will was startled. Natoncks was one of the Misquinnipack children he'd played with as a young boy. He shook his head. "He has mentioned no other Indian names at all, as far as I can remember."

"Think carefully, lad, as the future of this plantation may depend upon it. Wrack your mind. Are you certain?"

Will paused for a long moment before he answered. "Yes, sir, I am certain. And I don't think Squamiset is the type to be involved in any conspiracies—"

"Enough." Rockingham held up his hand for silence. "I take you at your word, Will, that your old Beelzebub has mentioned nothing to you about conspiracies. Still, the fact remains that you have spent a good amount of time alone in the forest with this warlock or sorcerer or *powwaw*—whatever you wish to call him. It is quite probable, whether you feel it or not, that you have been infected in some measure by his heathen demonism. So here's my judgment: you are to stay out of the forest. You are to leave the bounds of the palisade only with the express permission of your legal guardian here." He glanced up pointedly, and Overlock nodded.

"Moreover, for the foreseeable future, you are to report to the Meetinghouse four days per week in addition to your regular attendance on Thursdays and Sundays. You shall be observed sitting in silent contemplation, and the teachings of our faith shall be employed to root out the lingering spiritual impurities you have picked up in the course of your ill-advised adventuring. There now, you see? Not so terrible, do you agree? But I do have a final warning for you, Will Poole: the penalty for further disobedience will be not be so mild. Do I make myself clear?"

Will bowed his head. There was no point in arguing. He was grateful that he wasn't going to be whipped or publicly humiliated.

Rockingham reached for the tankard, took a last swallow, picked up his hat, and rose to his feet. "Goodman Overlock, I thank you for the excellent beer. I shall see both of you at the Meetinghouse for tomorrow's solemn event."

Will gave a halfhearted bow as Overlock saw their guest to the door while thanking him obsequiously for gracing their simple dwelling place with his distinguished and godly presence.

Afterward, alone with the steward at the supper table, Will was too angry to speak. There was little doubt that Overlock had been a good deal more observant than he'd let on: he'd played a key role in the Governor's discovery of Will's friendship with Squamiset. Beneath the steward's attitude of tactful concern, Will detected an undertone of triumph. Triumph that Will's recklessness had earned him an official rebuke. Triumph that Will had been brought to heel. Triumph that the Governor had refreshed himself with Overlock's own beer, in Overlock's own house. Because, for all practical purposes, it *was* Overlock's house, not Will's.

And the steward wasn't finished yet. "You won't have heard this," he announced as he lit the candles at the table, his small eyes glittering above his plump cheeks. "Earlier today your magical friend was apprehended and banished forever from this valley. In the process of dealing with him, Captain Hooker has arrested a young Misquinnipack who it turns out was at the Wethersfield Massacre."

Will stopped chewing to stare at his guardian. His supper settled like a lead weight to the bottom of his stomach.

Overlock continued, "It's said the brute murdered three Englishmen with a tomahawk at Wethersfield—three we *know* of, that is. God help us; there are almost certainly more." He sighed, shaking his head. "The young murderer is now in the gaol awaiting his final judgment day, which is scheduled for tomorrow, as his Excellency hinted, at the Meetinghouse."

"Which Misquinnipack is it?" Will asked. "Do you know his name?"

Overlock nodded. "Governor Rockingham mentioned that as well: Natoncks. Their king's son, I believe, although you know how it goes with these savages. They're all related to the king one way or another, it seems, for he keeps a great harem of wives."

"But that's impossible," Will said, incredulous. "Natoncks is *my* age. Wethersfield was four years ago. He would have been twelve. Captain Hooker has made a mistake."

Overlock shrugged, ladling himself another helping of stew. "So you know *this* savage too? Remarkable." Will nodded, distracted by memories. Moments later, he climbed the ladder to his sleeping berth and threw himself down on the straw-stuffed ticking. He lay on his back, staring up into the cramped darkness.

The clearest memory he had of Natoncks was a midsummer day when they'd both been about eight years old. Will had joined a group of Misquinnipack boys on a larking run through the forest on the far side of the river, the northwestern side, where the wilderness was uninterrupted by any settlement or road. It had poured rain the night before, yet the ground was not muddy, as he'd expected, but pleasantly dry, covered in absorbent layers of moss and leaf litter that made a springy surface to run across. They must have run for hours, through a forest of stony beech trunks and oaks and shagbark hickories, over rushing streams that cut through granite ledges slashed with glittering veins of quartz. They came to an ancient pine with a trunk so broad that eight boys could not encircle it with their arms, and this was the tree they decided to climb.

Looking up, Will couldn't see the crown, only the trunk with its branches spiraling up into the sky like Jack of the Beanstalk. Natoncks, a leader among the Misquinnipack boys, was the first to scale the tree. There were no branches on the lower trunk, and Natoncks climbed in a way that seemed impossible to Will, with his weight braced outward, searching for handholds in the furrowed bark. One by one the other boys followed up into the branches until only Will remained on the ground. Natoncks whistled, beckoning with his hand for Will to come up. "I can't," Will said in English, shaking his head. "I don't know how to climb that way."

Natoncks slid down the trunk and, wordlessly—for he spoke no English and Will spoke only a word or two of Algonkian—showed Will how to use his fingers to probe the rough bark for traction, how to lean out and brace his bare feet against the trunk. Will was clumsy compared to the Misquinnipack boys, and he almost toppled backward more than once. By the time he reached the lower branches his heart was clamoring, but he'd made it. He sat straddling a thick limb, catching his breath as the other boys swarmed high above him into the tree, nimble and carefree as squirrels.

Natoncks gave him a reassuring pat on the shoulder and started off. Will followed, trying not to think about the earth receding beneath his feet. The smell of pine was strong in his nostrils, and his hands were sticky with sap. But he soon began to feel more self-assured. There was a rhythm in the regular spacing of the branches. Climbing was easy if you didn't look down, he decided. If you didn't stop to think about what you were doing.

High in the tree, the boys clustered like jays on flimsy branches just below the crown, which towered above the rest of the canopy so that it was surrounded on all sides by empty air. Will hugged the swaying trunk with both arms. Natoncks glanced down from his perch and pointed to his left eye, a gesture the Misquinnipack used when they wished for someone to observe. Then he swept his free arm out beyond the dancing pine boughs.

Will raised his eyes and caught his breath. The forest north and west of New Meadow was much more vast than he'd imagined, an ocean of rolling hills cloaked with bright green hardwoods and darker conifers. Beyond the coastal hills lay a broad plain speckled with lakes and ponds that shimmered in the sun like mirrors. The Misquinnipack River unfurled northward in a long silver ribbon. Half a dozen waterfalls and white-water rapids were clearly visible, though they were oddly silent and immobile, as if distance could halt the flow of time.

Natoncks spoke to Will in Algonkian. Will didn't know the words, but he understood the meaning. As he gazed out over that wilderness, a weight lifted from his shoulders that he hadn't even known was there. He felt tiny—and at the same time as big as the sky.

Now, lying in the darkness in his too-small sleeping berth, he found it impossible to believe that the lithe and kindhearted boy who'd brought him up that pine tree could have taken part in the bloody raid at Wethersfield. The idea that Natoncks might soon be executed for this wrongheaded accusation made him feel ill. And now that Squamiset had been exiled, he had no one to turn to.

He made up his mind to speak to John Rockingham at the Meetinghouse tomorrow. He was in no position to ask for anything, but surely the Governor could be made to understand that this was a clear case of mistaken identity.

Six

New Meadow was among the more prosperous of the New England settlements, not because of any wealth hidden in the rocky forests or salt marshes on this stretch of coast, but for the simple reason that most of its residents had arrived with means in hand. They were milliners and woolen merchants, ship owners, and, as in the case of Thomas Poole, Will's father, the younger sons of noble families. Most were devout Puritans, their chief concern to be counted among the Saved, their most fervent desire to multiply their fortunes in the virgin soil of America. Their houses were capped with steep roofs of thatch or slate, anchored by ballast-brick chimneys, and brightened by windows of imported diamond-paned glass. It was a proper English village nervously toeing the edge of the American wilderness: quiet, self-contained, and armed to the teeth.

Following Divine Service, if the weather were favorable, the God-fearing colonists of New Meadow enjoyed lingering on the grass of the common. It was a chance to socialize, exchange gossip, and breathe a bit of fresh air after so many hours in the stuffy Meetinghouse.

On this mild Sunday afternoon in May, wishing to speak to the Governor, Will broke away from his guardian and set off after the plantation's leading citizen. Rockingham was strolling with his hands behind his back toward the gaol, a squat stone building across the common from the Meetinghouse. He was deep in conversation with Captain Hooker, the head of New Meadow's volunteer militia. Will caught up just as the two men reached the heavy oak door of the gaol. "Your Excellency, may I have a word?"

Rockingham turned to face him. Hooker turned, too, but the moment he recognized Will he glanced away and stood staring into the distance as he waited for the boy to finish his business.

"What is it, Will?" the Governor asked in patient tones, yet Will could see that he was annoyed by the interruption.

"The prisoner, sir. Natoncks. I knew him as a child. It's not possible that he took part in the Wethersfield massacre."

At this, Captain Hooker's pale grey eyes snapped back to Will. He started to say something, but the Governor held up a spider-fingered hand. He gazed coldly at Will. "Is it wise for you to insert yourself in this matter, Will? After what we discussed yesterday?"

Will colored. "I don't know how wise it is, sir, but in the interest of justice I really feel I must speak out. Natoncks is far too young to have been at the Wethersfield raid. I'm certain of it."

Hooker stared at him with unfiltered hatred. "You have no idea what you're saying, boy. I don't suppose you knew any of those who lost their lives at Wethersfield."

"No, sir, but—"

"Well, I did. I lost some dear friends in that massacre; they were slaughtered in their sleep. And I assure you that your old playmate is a remorseless murderer. Now, kindly be on your way."

Will stood his ground. "So he's not entitled to a trial?"

The expression that came into the Governor's blue eyes at that moment sent a shiver down Will's spine. "If I were you, Master Poole, I wouldn't push my luck. Do you take my meaning?"

Will stood there for a moment, arguments forming themselves and dying on his lips. These men were obviously not going to listen. A wave of nausea came over him, accompanied by the bleakest despair. "I hope you will be merciful," he said and turned to walk away over the common. But even as he said them he knew the words were futile. The Governor would not be merciful. And there was nothing Will could do.

That night as Will lay unsleeping in his berth, however, he realized that he had to do *something*. The whole chain of events was his fault. If he hadn't roused suspicions with his secretive trips to the forest, Rockingham would never have known that Squamiset was visiting. And if Hooker and his men hadn't gone to the Misquinnipack village to confront the old man, Natoncks would still be snoring peacefully under the bark of his parents' longhouse. He dearly wished he could talk to Squamiset. Perhaps if he went to the village, he could find out where the old man had gone or how to get a message to him.

It was nearly midnight. Overlock was most likely fast asleep. Feeling around in the dark, Will pulled on his clothes and shoes. He crept down the ladder and carefully lifted the latch to let himself out. The gate of the palisade was sealed, so the only way out of the village was by water. And the truth was, he'd never been a strong swimmer.

It was a still, moonless night. Small waves slapped against the planking. The harbor around the wharf was shallow enough to wade in, but it got deep quickly. Hopefully, if he waded straight toward the shore beyond the palisade, he wouldn't encounter water over his head. Gritting his teeth against the cold, he gingerly lowered himself down into the chest-deep brine. He waded out into the darkness, taking what he believed was a straight line toward a small beach beyond the eastern limit of the wall. The bottom was silted and mucky, and he had a few moments of worry that his feet would get stuck, but eventually his feet found the firm sand of the beach. Saltwater poured from the cuffs of his breeches and sloshed around in his stockings and shoes. He sat on the beach and took off his shoes, emptying out the muck.

The beach led to a tidal canal that ran along the northern wall of the palisade. Moving fast and keeping as low as possible, he made his way along the bank of this canal to the packed-earth cart track known as Neck Lane. At the track he turned right. This road led out past the clay pits and pastures to a bridge across the Misquinnipack River and then to a narrow footpath to the peninsula that held the Indian village.

He felt the drumbeats before he heard them: a steady, mournful thumping. Following the path, his waterlogged shoes squelching, he came to the spot where the river widened, opening to a long marshy delta as it flowed into the harbor. Beside it was a long meadow on the far end of which was the circular wall of stakes surrounding the Misquinnipack village. Will had been inside this wall once long ago. He still remembered what a shock it had been to see the Indians' bark hovels. Now, after his time with Squamiset, he understood that his concern had been misplaced. The Misquinnipack were rich enough in their own way without grand immovable houses and brick chimneys and cartloads of imported wooden furniture.

He caught himself just in time to avoid stumbling into the militiamen Captain Hooker had posted at the entrance to the village. There were half a dozen of them clustered like beetles in the shadows, guarding the entry of the palisade. Heart knocking in his chest, Will stayed frozen in place for as long as he dared. The guards didn't seem to have detected him in the darkness. He backed away slowly, then turned and slipped into the deep shadows at the fringe of the meadow.

A hedge of dense scrub separated the grass from the sea. Creeping along it in the darkness he came to an opening, which proved to be a path leading down through the scrub to the beach. He walked along the shoreline for a time. Soon he came to a large midden of discarded clam and oyster shells. Beyond this, a narrow path led him back up to the meadow and the far side of the palisade wall. From within the village, the mournful drums rolled on. He assumed it had something to do with Natoncks.

Taking off his waterlogged shoes felt good. He stood and ran his hands over the vertical logs of the palisade. This wall wasn't anywhere near as high or massive as the New Meadow palisade, and there were plenty of knots and bulges. Remembering how Natoncks and his friends had used their fingers and bare feet to scramble up the lower trunk of that huge pine on that long ago day, he set about trying to scale the wall.

It wasn't easy. Several times he lost his grip and tumbled backward into the dewy grass. Finally, he managed to clamber high enough to grip the sharp point of one of the palings. He scrabbled for a foothold, panting and hoisting his weight upward so that he caught a glimpse of the nearest Misquinnipack houses, a file of bark-covered domes illuminated by flickering firelight. A strange emotion came over him. It was as if he'd arrived home after a long journey. Despite the risks, he was glad he'd come.

Then a callused hand grabbed his ankle.

"Got ye," came the satisfied whisper. A quick tug and the ground rose up to meet him. Will hit the ground so hard that it knocked his wind out. As he struggled for breath, the militiaman knelt on his chest, holding a cutlass to his throat.

"Got him here!" the volunteer cried hoarsely. Will recognized the voice: it was Caleb Stonehill, the blacksmith. His comrades came thumping across the grass, their boat-helmeted heads leaning in to blot out the stars. One of the men sparked the pan of his musket and held the sizzling weapon close to Will's face. The bright light blinded him.

"By God, if it isn't young Will Poole!" Will recognized this voice, too: it belonged to Jack Little, the stork-limbed watchman who had once been his tutor. "Gone over to the savages, have ye, boy?" Little's tone was neither understanding nor kind. Nor were the callused hands that jerked him to his feet and led him back toward the English village.

Squamiset sat on the edge of a cliff on the high sandstone ridge that the Musqunnipuck called Koweonk Mogosketomp, the Sleeping Giant.

Stretching out below the cliff was a great sweep of coastal forest, and beyond that a silvery strip of ocean enclosed by a long finger of land that his people called Montauk and the Dutch called Lange Eylandt. Beyond that, the crimson face of the sun peered over the horizon.

"Come, my old friend," Squamiset murmured in a voice audible only to himself. "I need your counsel." It was dawn, his second day on the cliff, the third after the capture of young Natoncks. So far the sky had shown only ravens and vultures and the smaller birds, moths, and dragonflies that flitted in and out of his field of vision. It was the osprey he needed.

The sun climbed higher, warming his shivering body. Meanwhile, hunger and pokeweed worked on his mind, and he found himself wandering in the world of memory. The ship's master who had kidnapped him those many seasons past was called Wight. He had a waxed mustache, a stiff black beard, and tiny round eyes that danced merrily one moment and shone with cruel calculation the next. His crewmen had urged the curious young Mannomoyiks to climb a rope ladder up onto the ship, and four, including Squamiset, had been bold enough to try it.

Captain Wight called for a cask of burnt Madeira wine and invited the young adventurers to his cabin, which had a row of windows overlooking the sea. The young men were fascinated by the glass, which was like pond ice, only warm to the touch. Wight and his mate used gestures to communicate, passing around mirrors and glittering strings of beads for the young Mannomoyiks to admire as they drank more and more of the wine. The walls of the cabin began to spin. At a certain moment Wight must have given a signal to the mate. The mate called out an order and a gang of crewmen streamed in to seize Squamiset and his three friends. They wrestled them down into the dark bowels of the ship, where six Algonkians from other parts of the coast already lay chained to heavy iron rings in the floor. These prisoners were sick with fear. They told the new arrivals that they were all to be carried across the sea, where the coat-men planned to stew them alive and feed them to their king.

The memory vision was interrupted by a shrill cry. Squamiset gazed out at the air beyond the cliff. The osprey came soaring in from the southwest. It flapped its wings deftly and perched on a beech branch. The morning sun shone on its dark wing feathers, on the white head with its vivid black eye-stripe and the curved black beak. Its yellow eyes fixed him in a shrewd gaze. "Greetings, old one." Squamiset's voice came out in a croak. His hands trembled.

The osprey looked him over scornfully. *You are weak, Mannomoyik. It is fortunate you were not born with wings. You would not last an hour above the treetops.*

Squamiset filled his long clay pipe with pokeweed and used an ember from the small fire he'd been keeping to light the pipe. "Where should I take these young men?"

The osprey cocked its head. A translucent membrane slid down over its eye, causing it to appear strangely absent for a moment before the intense sidelong gaze resumed. *East, over the sea. To the island your people used to call Far-Away-Among-the-Waves. You have relations there who will welcome you.*

Squamiset nodded. He remembered a young cousin, the son of his mother's brother, who'd taken it into his mind to set off to cross the ocean in a *mishoon*. This was long ago, years before the English had come. After he'd paddled out to sea, a violent storm had arisen; everyone had assumed that the boy had drowned. "So my cousin lives on?"

He has fathered three generations. The island is distant and protected from discovery by shoals and swirling currents. The English have not drawn it on their maps. It will make an excellent hiding place.

"I fear things will not go easy for my friends in the village when I leave."

Your fear is well-founded. But you must undertake this journey.

Squamiset smoked the pipe, exhaling a cloud of smoke, which lingered for a moment before spiraling and dissipating in the breeze. He'd always assumed that Far-Away-Among-the-Waves was only a legend, a mythical island of bountiful harvests and tall, sun-bronzed men who spoke the language of fish and rode whales the way the Englishmen rode horses. He supposed that getting there would be a great challenge. On the open ocean a pleasant breeze could become a howling wind, and great storms could arise with little warning. A *mishoon* was a fragile vessel for such a crossing, even without the risks presented by the shoals and currents. Visions of the future were always conditional. Each moment had to be survived in order to reach the next.

He stayed where he was a long time, smoking the pipe, his back cradled in a curve of sun-warmed rock. Then he knocked the cinders out on the stone, scattered the remains of the fire, and got to his feet.

Seven

The gaol cell was dark and reeked of mold. The only furnishing on the straw-covered floor was a fresh round of elm, most likely sawn from the same stout trunk felled to make Natoncks' chopping block. Days had passed since Will's arrest; he'd lost count of how many. His clothes smelled of mildew and he couldn't stop shivering. Sometimes he slipped into a kind of delirium, hallucinating that he was in another place— working in a garden in sunlight, climbing to the crow's nest of a ship, overhearing sobs in a firelit hall—and when he came back into himself the cell seemed even smaller and darker than before. No sunlight came in through the single recessed window to warm the heavy stone walls. He had nothing to read, nothing to write, nothing to do but lament his fate and that of Natoncks, who was most likely imprisoned in the gaol's adjoining cell, although the walls were too thick to attempt any kind of communication.

His only escape was sleep. Twice he experienced the old familiar dream of flying—of walking along and casting himself up into the wind—and the dream was even more bittersweet than usual because of the conditions he encountered when he awoke. His sense of being trapped, only an abstract feeling before, was now as real as the stone walls that closed him off from the world. The second time he dreamed of flying, the wilderness unfolded beneath him, a great rolling tapestry of hills and trees and ponds and streams. He traced the topography with his flight, avid for the fragrant air, the evocative sounds of insect song, birdsong, wolfsong. When he awoke, he found himself shivering in the moldy straw on the floor of his unlit cell. Out of the darkness a new wave of frightening hallucinations came to visit him, one after the other: a tangled pile of skeletons laced with rotting clothes; himself chained underwater, incapable of swimming or breathing; a ghostly green face leaning in close, speaking words into his ear whose meaning was lost in a trail of bubbles.

These delusions, these waking hallucinations, were much worse than dreams. They felt as real as a finger in his eye, and there was no avoiding them. Doubt whispered in his ear. A wheedling logic tugged at the mildewed sleeves of his doublet. He was imprisoned because he'd been tricked by Satan. If he turned his back on the Devil—firmly and forever—the omnipotent Lord would embrace him.

One night—or at least he thought it was night—he was sitting awake with his back to the cold stone wall, hoping that sleep would descend to relieve him, when he heard the hooting of an owl. It was near at hand, seemingly just outside the recessed slit window, which was strange, for there were no trees on the common on which such a large bird could perch. It hooted again, a low, confidential sound. Perhaps it was circling the common, scouring the grass for field mice. Or perhaps it was just another of his hallucinations. He pressed his eyes closed and massaged his eyelids with his fingertips, willing sleep to come.

With the next hoot he sprang to his feet, heart pounding. He strode over to the window, crouching beneath the gaol's low ceiling. Outside the slit he could make out just a hint of silvery moonlight. "Who's there?" he whispered. "Is it really an owl? Or is it you, Satan, returning to torment me?"

"One more guess," said a droll voice.

"Squamiset!"

"Greetings, Will."

Will leaned against the cold stone beside the window. "It was a terrible mistake for you to come," he said. "If the Governor catches you he will cut off your head, along with poor Natoncks.'"

A moment's silence and the familiar voice came through the slit, filled with a confidence that was like a bracing tonic to Will. "I am here to set you free, Will. But if you come along with me, you will never again be allowed to live among the English. You must think about that."

"Why would you do this? And wouldn't I be a burden to you on your travels?"

"We are to undertake a journey together, Will. I have foreseen it. It is my destiny."

Will shivered, wracked by doubt. The walls of the gaol were designed to be indestructible. His cell was sealed by a door of reinforced oak. And how could he be sure that this conversation was even real? Nevertheless, at this moment, Will thought he would give up just about anything for his freedom. He might even sell his soul to the Devil, because burning in Hell couldn't be worse than shivering away in this mildewed cell as the rest of the world basked in summer. On the other hand, hallucinatory or no, Squamiset's words were true. There was no doubt about what escaping into the wilderness would mean. Only months ago an English fur trader at Fort Saybrook had been hanged for the crime of taking a Pequot wife. If Will were to flee with Squamiset, a known sorcerer, he would forever be considered a traitor to his faith. He would be hunted, and if he were to be recaptured—well, he didn't want to think about that.

"Can you free Natoncks as well?" he asked.

There was no response. He waited a moment. "Squamiset?"

But Will could feel the desertedness on other side of the wall, and the bitter taste of disappointment rose up in his throat. He lay down in the moldy straw and tried to sleep. He'd given up trying to figure out if the hallucinations were symptoms of approaching madness or tricks of the Devil designed to ensnare him. It hardly mattered. But this latest one seemed exceptionally cruel.

The house was quiet without Will. James felt sorry for the boy, but he had authored his own fall from grace. It wasn't as if he hadn't been warned—repeatedly—and despite the strain of recent events, James couldn't help taking a measure of satisfaction in the happy turn his own fortunes had taken. Will Poole's disgrace may have thrown James's competence as a guardian into a questionable light, but the important people—most essentially Governor John E. Rockingham—understood that James had taken every conceivable measure to head it off.

He still had Zeke Poole to contend with, when and if that brash young seafarer returned from his latest merchant voyage. But for now, James controlled more than enough funds to secure his own future. The Governor thought well of him. Now that Will Poole was imprisoned by plantation officials, it was only natural that James's term of servitude should expire. And the best thing of all? On more than one recent occasion Rockingham had hinted that a certain hundred-acre plot in the fertile common lands south and west of the village, where an aggressive program of woodcutting had set the wilderness in retreat, would soon become available. That James might become the owner of his own hundred-acre plot was a prospect beyond his wildest dreams.

More immediately, there was the savage's execution to witness. It was to be a grim demonstration of Divine Justice, although—predictably—the forces of Satan seemed to be mounting some resistance: the event had been scheduled and then delayed for two days running by a number of disturbing events. At dawn on the first day, a multitude of white caterpillars the size of thumb joints had emerged from the ground to attack the plantation's crops. The entire English population (excepting Will Poole, of course) had gone out to pick the disgusting creatures from the branches of the fruit trees and the tender shoots of corn, wheat, and beans. On the second morning, just as the citizens of New Meadow had gathered on the common to see the Divine Will accomplished, there had arisen an ominous roaring, and the sky had grown dark with a vast migration of passenger pigeons. The birds had come in such numbers that they were like the souls of the dead of all ages past, and the sun had been hidden from view for a full six hours. So many pigeons had flapped down from the sky that they'd had to land upon each other's backs, and their weight had caused strong green branches to crack and fall.

When the birds had finally moved on—there were far too many to shoot or drive away—the fields, gardens, and orchards of New Meadow were left desolate and covered in layers of white bird excrement. But the leaves of the wild forest trees, beyond the cultivated fields, had been untouched by either caterpillars or birds, confirming what many had already suspected: these were not natural creatures but messengers of Satan, mischievous pests sent from Hell to delay the execution of his slave.

On the third morning, the doleful bell of the Meetinghouse rang eight times. The people of New Meadow gathered on their soiled common. Two dozen armed volunteers manned the watchtowers to prevent any trouble from the local savages or their more populous allies to the east, the Nehantics. The sky was filled with low grey clouds that seemed to press down upon the roofs of the houses around the green. A stiff northwest wind had blown in, causing the fragile warmth of May to recoil in a crouching March-like rawness. The crowd let off a low, restless murmur. The strange events of the last few days had set everyone on edge.

James wore his new silk hose and the fine black doublet he'd ordered from Liverpool. He'd had a few last-minute doubts about donning such expensive clothing, but most of the other planters—and all the gentlemen—had also put on their finest. The crowd was sea of black velvet and silk, with the occasional slash of burgundy or emerald green, and James was relieved to see that his outfit was a perfectly tasteful choice. He loved the expensive feel of the fabric, how firmly and softly the hose clasped his calves, how the well-cut doublet whispered over his linen shirt when he moved. Between the crowd and the Meetinghouse steps a rectangle of ground had been kept open by the pikemen, their blades and helmets glinting dully in the grey light. In the center of this open area, the Governor's men had placed a massive round of fresh-cut elm. James stared at this makeshift executioner's block with a mix of distaste and fascination. It was to be New Meadow's first execution.

The Governor had mandated that Will Poole was to witness the execution. James looked him over, careful to avoid meeting the young man's eyes. He was bound at the wrists, and an armed militiaman stood on either side. He looked pale and exhausted, begrimed and shivering with a few pieces of straw in his hair. But there was a defiant set to his jaw. Clearly, the boy was not remorseful—not desperate, as of yet, to seek the omnipotent Lord's grace. James was hopeful, however, that the act of Divine Justice they were about to witness, followed by more confinement of an as yet undecided duration, would do wonders for the boy's mutinous spirit. In any case, he thought as he allowed his gaze to wander elsewhere, Will Poole was no longer his legal concern.

Four guards brought the savage out and forced him to his knees before the chopping block. His long black hair was matted and, just like Will's, flecked with pieces of straw from the floor of the gaol. He was a muscular youth with a swarthy chiseled face that James supposed might have been handsome had it belonged to an Englishman. Will had said that this was one of the Misquinnipack boys he'd used to play with on the riverbank. James remembered them as slim, disquieting shadows darting in and out of the trees. He had no qualms whatsoever about witnessing this one's beheading. He was a known murderer and a likely minion of the Devil, and James believed that he could see the spiritual corruption in his eyes. Perhaps it would provide a salutary warning to the other savages. Perhaps they would think twice in the future about questioning God's Divine Laws or attacking New Meadow's dedicated captain of militia.

John Rockingham came out from the Meetinghouse and stood on the raised porch facing the assembly. His Excellency was clad in black with a flowing cape and a magnificent embroidered sable doublet with slashed sleeves the same color as his silver mustache and V-shaped beard. He looked over the crowd, and for a moment his piercing blue eyes came to rest on James himself. The great man gave a slight conspiratorial nod, and James colored deeply, stirred by the honor of being singled out in public by such a man. Red-bearded Captain Daniel Hooker, a career soldier who'd fought in the religious wars in Bohemia and the Low Countries, stationed himself behind the kneeling Natoncks. He was flanked by seven pikemen in corselets and steel-brimmed helmets.

For a moment James was disoriented, as if he'd just arrived home after a long journey in a foreign land. He'd seen executions before, back in England, but it was hard to believe this act of Righteousness and Justice was about to occur within the humble confines of the New Meadow plantation. It made him feel solemn, and a little sad.

The drummer pounded out a low tattoo. Captain Hooker pulled a black executioner's hood over his thick head, and an assistant handed Hooker a double-bladed woodsman's axe. A rippling silence fell across the crowd. A flock of ravens had slipped in to perch on the crooked Meetinghouse roof and gazed down at the crowd like scornful, black-robed judges. James's breath came faster. The excitement rose in his chest.

The Governor cleared his throat, preparing to speak to the crowd. But at that moment, the ravens flew up in a mass of raucous cawing and flapping black wings. The crowd gasped, and a clumsy man in front of James stepped back into him, causing him to lose his balance. It took him a moment to recover, and at first he couldn't make out what was happening. Then he saw it.

On the very peak of the Meetinghouse roof stood a hideous figure: huge, naked, and scarlet, heavily muscled and built like a man but half again as large. Shiny black horns—long and twisted inward like those of an ancient billy goat—grew out of a warty vermillion forehead. Leering white eyes bulged from their sockets, like those of a monstrous blind toad.

Recovering from its collective shock, the crowd began to scatter. James stood for a moment, transfixed. The monster leapt down from the roof, landing on the common in a predatory crouch. It licked its lips with a long black tongue, and its arrow-pointed tail twitched like a cat's. James, succumbing to the generalized panic, turned on his heels and fled.

It took Will a moment to realize that this creature with vacant eyes and twisting horns was Squamiset. If he hadn't already seen some of what his elderly friend was capable of, he would never have believed that such a vivid image could be conjured up in the eyes of all those watching.

He stayed where he was as the terrified citizens of New Meadow scattered to their houses to shutter their windows and bar their doors. Within a few moments Will, the Devil, and Natoncks were the only ones left on the common. The Devil brandished a knife, and with a few quick strokes cut the cords binding first Natoncks and then Will. There was a slight softening around the figure's outlines as the illusion lost strength, then a rippled blur, like something glimpsed through a windowpane on a rainy day. Soon the Devil was replaced by the figure of Squamiset himself: the old friendly face with its great hooked nose, the faded horse-man's jacket, the gold hoops glinting in the dull grey light. He gestured for Will and Natoncks to follow and set off at a run for the gap in the palisade down by the harbor.

Will had to exert himself to keep up—both Squamiset and Natoncks were fast runners—but at the same time he found himself reveling in ordinary sensations: the air on his cheeks, the bumble-bees buzzing, the apple blossoms on the breeze. As they ran past his house the door swung open. Will cried out a warning, and Squamiset reacted swiftly, turning and dropping to one knee with his bow bent.

Natoncks stood beside the old man, prepared for a fight. Overlock leaned against the doorframe like a merchant taking the air on a leisurely afternoon. It was a wonder that he'd recovered his calm so quickly, but lately Will had been discovering many things about the steward that surprised him.

"Sometimes I think I have the second sight, Will," Overlock said. "A little voice inside my head whispered that Satan himself would be passing by my door." The steward sighed, shaking his head regretfully. "I tried to counsel you wisely, Will; the Lord knows I did. Out of loyalty to your father—God rest his soul—I did my best to finish your education. In addition to providing a secure and well-stocked home, I've tried to protect you from Satan's wiles and from your own errors." He nodded in the direction of Squamiset and Natoncks. "Obviously, in these last respects I have failed."

"Are you going to raise the alarm?"

"To judge by the looks of him, your sorcerer would put an arrow through my lungs if I tried that. In any case, far be it from me to stand in your way any longer. You've chosen to give up your inheritance, and I plan to use it wisely. God and the spirit of your departed father know that I have discharged my duties as well as I could."

"I'm sure my father's spirit, wherever it is, sees you exactly as you are, Overlock."

"You can't run forever," Will's former guardian warned in an icy voice. "When the Governor catches you, do not doubt it: you shall be put to death. And barring a complete repentance, you shall burn in Hell for all eternity."

"If there *is* a Hell, I won't be surprised to meet you there."

"Ha! Godspeed, then." The servant mimed the act of washing his hands, stepped inside the house, and latched the door behind him. Will stared at the closed door of his childhood home. The magnitude of the decision he'd made began to sink in.

Squamiset relaxed his bow and slipped the arrow back into its quiver. The baying of dogs sounded from the market square; it was time to go. They jogged down to the landing, where a *mishoon* awaited them.

Eight

Will awoke with sore feet and a spirit of fiery exuberance. It was the dawn of a bright summer day. The scent of wild roses filled the air, mingling with hemlock needles and dew-covered grass. Songbirds declaimed their intricate songs from the treetops, and he was free.

They'd paddled the *mishoon* across the harbor to the far side of the river mouth and abandoned it. Squamiset had tossed him a bundle containing, among other things, a buckskin hunting smock and a pair of the leather slippers that the Indians called *moccasins*. Will was happy to shed his old doublet and oxhide shoes; Squamiset made him bury them under a mossy log. The three of them had set off at a steady jog along the much-used coastal trail. When darkness fell they'd slept on beds of hemlock boughs deep in the forest. Numb and exhausted, Will had had no trouble slipping into a deep and dreamless sleep.

Now it was morning, time to move. They continued eastward along the coast, through boulder-strewn forests and tidal marshes riddled with streams and sinkholes. Their pace today was somewhat slower, less of a run and more of a fast walk. They stopped only to drink from clear streams and eat parched corn, which Squamiset poured into the young men's cupped hands from a leather pouch. Sometimes, strolling along a pebble beach or wading barefoot through the black muck of a salt marsh, they glimpsed the flashing sails of English or Dutch merchant sloops, and Will felt the first stirrings of doubt. There were English forts and plantations all along this coast. True, it was easy enough to detect such places and detour inland to avoid them. The ground was trampled, and the streams were muddy. The dung of cattle, sheep, and swine lay scattered on the ground, and whole swaths of forest had been felled, axed stumps poking up through the grassy earth like broken bones from flesh. But Governor Rockingham was a well-known figure in these settlements. He had many allies, and it was likely that word of the recent events in New Meadow had already spread. So far there had been no sign of pursuit—no shouting in the distance, no baying of hounds. But this couldn't last. And Will had no idea where the old man was taking them. He didn't feel like asking questions, however. Despite the aches in his legs and feet, he desired nothing more than to keep moving. The trail exerted a mindless, irresistible allure.

That evening they camped on a high slab of granite overlooking a pebble beach and the glittering blue ocean beyond. The slab received steady breezes coming off the ocean, so the fugitives weren't bothered by mosquitoes or flies, yet they were snug and hidden from anyone passing on the landward side by a dense wall of bayberry scrub. Will and Natoncks gathered driftwood for a fire, which Squamiset kindled with a flint and a pinch of touchwood. As the fire crackled to life, Squamiset told Will to keep it going while he and Natoncks went off to hunt for food. Despite himself, Will felt a twinge of jealousy that Squamiset had chosen Natoncks rather than himself as a hunting partner. But it only made sense: Natoncks had been an accomplished hunter since childhood, and Will was still a novice.

They returned shortly with handfuls of plump shorebirds. Will helped pluck them, and they basted the birds on sharpened green sticks. The three travelers enjoyed a hearty and delicious meal as the setting sun painted the surf with highlights of magenta and rose. Afterward, Will's curiosity finally won out, and he asked about their destination.

Squamiset wiped his hands on his grease-stained leggings. "There's an island, Will, far out to sea. English ships have never visited there, and it does not appear on their maps. It will be a safe haven for us, at least for a time."

"I see," Will said. This was a surprise. He'd been assuming that they would head north at some point and west into the vast unknown interior of the continent. He'd envisioned high granite mountaintops and roaring white-water rivers. "Is it a large island?"

"It is said a man can walk across it in half a day. From what I understand, although it is surrounded and protected by dangerous shoals and currents, the waters on the north shore of the island are calm and pleasant."

"And the people who live there will welcome us?"

"I believe so. Apparently I have a cousin who lives there."

"But you've never been there yourself."

"No. It's not an easy journey to get there."

"I see."

Squamiset's gaze took on a sudden intensity. "Do you?"

"Well, what choice do we have?"

"Correct. But what I mean is this: do you see our crossing? Have you glimpsed an ocean voyage?"

Will raked his mind, but there was little he could remember of the hallucinations. In retrospect, they were just a montage of half-forgotten daydreams. It was the feelings the visions provoked that lingered, rather than the visions themselves: disorientation, confusion, alarm.

When dusk came they let the fire die so that the campsite wouldn't be visible to English ships offshore. Squamiset lit a pipe of some peppery herb, and Will used his hunting knife to whittle a howling wolf from a piece of driftwood. Natoncks seemed content to sit in silence, staring out over the ocean.

Darkness fell. The only sounds were the subdued roar of the breakers and the sizzle of pebbles as the surf combed itself back into the sea.

· · ·

Dawn. In the cool breeze off the ocean, Will awoke shivering, a queasiness deep in his gut. The idea of setting off across the wide ocean for an island that was supposedly so well-protected by treacherous shoals that English mapmakers had yet to discover it—and that might, it must be said, not even exist—had begun to strike him as more than a little foolish. Perhaps it would be safer to seek refuge on ground they knew to be solid, instead of on an island in the middle of the hungry ocean that might prove not to exist at all.

They had to keep moving, though; he did understand that. As long as they remained on this coast, they could be captured at any given moment. *Do not doubt it: you shall be put to death*, Overlock had said. The image of himself twisting at the end of a rope—Will Poole, face blue and bloated, flies buzzing all around—but no. It wasn't a vivid image in his mind—not yet. If he allowed it to become so, he would surely go mad.

Squamiset scowled as he sifted handfuls of parched corn powder into Will's and Natoncks's open palms, and Will could see that the old man was in no mood for further questions or meaningless talk. It was time to move. They resumed their journey east along the coast in dew-drenched silence, striding quickly along a trail that wound through an open forest interspersed with mossy dells. The bottoms of Will's feet were slightly bruised from the impact of stones and roots through the soles of the pliable *moccasins*, but he couldn't imagine how blistered they would have been if he'd tried to come all this way in stiff English shoes.

As on previous days, they met no others on the trail. Around midday they came to an abandoned Nehantic village, a sad, haunted place perched on a bluff overlooking the ocean. It was bounded on the landward side by an unusual rock formation, a jagged crescent of pointed boulders as tall as houses, like colossal shark's teeth erupting from the grass. The village was quickly being reclaimed by the forest, which was filling it in with sumac and blackberry scrub, but it had once been home to a sizable group of people. Most of the dwellings had collapsed. Those left standing were empty scaffolds, like the rib cages of whales or elephants, with a few strips of bark left twisting in the breeze.

A sudden furious flapping caused Will to jump back. A flock of ravens rose up from behind one of the boulders, careening upward like an explosion of black ghosts. Will shuddered. The hairs on the back of his neck stood up, and he was overtaken by a quick flurry of visions. A sunny afternoon with the whole band gathered. The men repairing fishnets and the women spreading corn on reed mats to dry in the sun. Laughing children chasing each other around the boulders, one of them, remarkably, with blue eyes and white-blond hair like a Scandinavian. A feast in the village center, with a roaring fire and drums beating and a group of young men singing like the wind, like wolves, like seals, like coyotes. The swift intensity of these vision fragments staggered him. He had to sit down just to recover his balance.

He'd heard the stories; everyone had. Plagues of smallpox sweeping the coast in advance of the English colonists. Entire villages wiped out. Others decimated to the point where there weren't enough survivors left to bury the dead. Governor Rockingham believed the plagues were Divine Providence, God's way of clearing the land for those who had been saved by His Grace. Will found it impossible to think that such horrors could be the work of Divine Providence. He could see no bones or skulls among the ruined dwellings. But then he did not wish to look too closely.

Squamiset took a handful of pokeweed from a pouch. He crumbled it into the breeze, chanting a low-voiced prayer. Then they moved along.

Aside from parched corn, they ate nuts and berries, and at night they slept on beds of thick green moss. Once they stopped to lure speckled trout from a tea-colored stream, using a line made from the pounded fibers of cedar bark and a bone hook baited with grasshoppers. When they could find no more grasshoppers, Natoncks tied a piece of duck feather onto the hook to make it look like a grasshopper. Will was amazed: it worked just as well. "The trout see what they want to see," Squamiset explained, noticing Will's surprise. "In this respect, trout are much like people."

When they came to the wind-tossed expanse of Narragansett Bay, Squamiset and Natoncks went off in search of a vessel to take them across it. Will remained with the bundles, hidden inside a dense stand of cedars, for there was an English settlement on an island at the mouth of the bay. The cedar grove was a decent hiding place, but not, as it turned out, decent enough.

Squamiset and Natoncks had been gone for an hour or more. Will rested his back against a cedar's fibrous bark, fidgeting with the round-lobed needles. He was in a sour mood. It only made sense that Natoncks should be chosen to go with Squamiset; two strange Indians would arouse less suspicion than one strange Indian and an English youth dressed like an Indian. But, once again, he felt left out. He closed his eyes. Just as he was drifting off, he heard something crashing through the underbrush. He sat up, heart pounding. These clumsy footfalls did not belong to a forest animal. And they certainly didn't belong to Natoncks or Squamiset.

"Ho there! Why, I nearly stepped on you, boy!" The Englishman towered over him, red-faced, bug-eyed, and profusely sweating. He was outfitted for hunting in a leather jerkin and a red wool cap, a powder horn slung over his shoulder and a trumpet-barreled fowling piece held loosely in one hand. Will got to his feet, brushing off his backside.

"Good day, sir. Just taking a nap here." He tried to make his voice breezy and unconcerned, but he could see that it was not convincing. Will was a stranger on this stretch of the coast, and he'd clearly been hiding. Moreover, he was dressed in deerskin and Indian *moccasins*. None of this was normal.

Moving very slowly, as if this stranger were a grouse that he could spook, causing it to fly away, the hunter raised the fowling piece and aimed the gaping barrel at the center of Will's chest. "Unarmed, are ye? Where are your companions—the old witch and the young assassin?"

Will's heart sank. His worst fears were realized: word of their escape had preceded them along the coast. "Come now, sir," he said in reasonable tones. "You must have mistaken me for someone else. I'm just passing through all alone, and I was only"—Will glanced around, wracking his brain—"stopping here to gather mushrooms."

A malicious grin spread across the Englishman's florid face. "Mushrooms, is it? You'd better stick with me then, boy. I know where the best mushrooms are to be found in this area. Keep your hands in the air, though. Come out of there slowly. There's a good man."

The hunter took three steps backward, keeping the musket trained. Will hesitated, scanning the forest for a way to escape.

"Don't try it," the Englishman warned. Will came out of the cedars with his hands up. There was a strange tingling in his fingers. The hunter's unsympathetic eyes bulged as he jerked the blunderbuss in the direction of the water. "Lead the way, young heretic. I'm right behind you."

Will walked in a haze of dread as the Englishman directed him with the trumpet barrel down a well-trodden path along the shore of the bay. The hunter called out, and other English voices answered. Their calls grew louder as they approached through the forest; Will knew he had to make a run for it, but one shot from the blunderbuss would put a quick end to him. They were passing under a broad-branched oak when a dreadful moaning stopped them in their tracks. Will's reflexes took over; he threw himself on the ground and rolled over a tangle of roots and rocks to the side of the trail, where he took shelter behind an oak trunk and braced himself for the report of the blunderbuss.

The Englishman no longer noticed Will, however, because he was staring horror-struck up into the lowest branches of the oak. A strange figure sat with his legs casually dangling, staring down at the newcomers. The figure was strange because it appeared to be precisely that of the hunter himself, with the identical doublet, hose, broad falling collar, and wide-brimmed felt hat. But there were two important differences: the figure's skin had the lifeless grey pallor of a corpse, and the eyes staring down from the oak branch had no pupils, being blank and white as if they had rolled up into its skull.

Will shuddered with dread and revulsion despite his overwhelming relief. Squamiset had outdone himself. The illusion was horrid. The figure's pallid skin was transparent like the shell of a pupating caterpillar, with something green and sickly and awful slowly pulsing beneath it. And it got worse. The figure reached up and twisted off its own head, held it up, and dropped it to the ground, where it landed with a plunk at the feet of the English hunter.

The man gasped. Cringing back, he lost his balance and tumbled onto the leaf litter, losing his grip on the blunderbuss. The head was pale and greenish but fully recognizable with its blond beard and unseeing, bulged-out eyes, which were as lifeless and white as boiled eggs. Will could only imagine the Englishman's terror. He let out a choked sob, struggled to his feet, and ran. A few moments later his screams, and the increasingly alarmed shouts of his companions, echoed out over Narragansett Bay.

"We have located a *mishoon*," Squamiset announced matter-of-factly, swinging down from the oak branch. The illusion faded, although it took a moment for the Englishman's clothing to disappear and Squamiset's own head and face to resume their normal solidity and color. He bent to pick up the Englishman's severed head, which turned out to be a large winter squash.

Natoncks strode out of the woods bearing a cloth bundle, which he unrolled to reveal half a dozen dark green cucumbers and a mound of fresh beans. "And we shall eat well tonight."

· · ·

For the next two days they traveled east and north, moving as quickly as possible. There was no question now that they were hunted. Sometimes they could hear the baying of dogs in the distance. One night, from their well-concealed camp on an island in a cattail swamp at a river mouth, they spied a search party of helmeted militiamen crowded into three torchlit pinnaces.

The trail was more sand than dirt now, and the forest was scrubby dwarf oak and undernourished pitch pine. According to Squamiset, they'd crossed over onto the sandy hook of land the English called Cape Cod. For obvious reasons they stayed off the open beaches and kept to the relative shelter of the forest, but the ocean's salt essence was in the wind, and they could often hear the roar of surf. Will tried to keep himself from dwelling on the dangerous crossing that they were about to attempt, but he no longer questioned the wisdom of doing so. The baying dogs and searching torches made it clear that there was no alternative.

One morning they came to a pond capped by an unbroken layer of emerald lily pads. Squamiset and Natoncks stripped off their clothing, and in the next moment they knifed into the pond, their lean bodies raising scarcely a ripple as the lily pads closed in after them. Will stood on the shore, fidgeting worriedly. It didn't seem like the most appealing place for a swim or the best moment for it. But there hadn't been time to protest.

In a moment Squamiset emerged, strands of pondweed draped alongside his thin silver braids. The lily pads parted a few yards away, and Natoncks sputtered up to the surface. Between them, slowly, a length of shiny black wood floated up, and Will finally understood. It was a *mishoon*. Gingerly, he waded into the pond to help his two friends haul it out. It wasn't a large dugout, but it was extremely heavy. Even with three of them pushing and pulling, it was a monumental struggle to drag it up onto the bank.

They built a bonfire to dry it. It was an elegantly made boat, long and slender, and there was a detailed design of a sharp-beaked osprey carved into the prow. Squamiset had made it himself, he said. He'd dragged it out onto the ice and piled it full of rocks to send it to the bottom, where it had lain until he and Natoncks had swum down to lift out the rocks. Will found it hard to believe that such a small and delicate vessel could be seaworthy.

Natoncks and Will kept the fire banked while Squamiset whittled the first paddle from the trunk of a recently downed cedar. The boat had been underwater so long that it took two days of constant fire to dry it. Then they oiled it with rendered raccoon fat and dragged it several hundred yards south to the edge of an estuary that led to the open sea. They made camp on the grassy bank. Will and Squamiset built a cooking fire while Natoncks waded off into the brackish tidewater, returning with a shirt load of quahogs. They ate the smaller ones raw, using their knives to pry the shells open, and set the larger ones on rocks by the fire to smoke. The fresh clams were delicious: briny and cool, like flavorful morsels of the ocean itself.

Afterward, they sat in silence and stared at the fire. Will's mood was fretful. Images kept coming back to him of his mother's burial at sea—the sailcloth envelope that she'd been sewn into with a cannonball at her feet. A young boy at the time, Will had cried as he'd watched the strange envelope spiral down and disappear into the clear green depths—the depths of the same deadly expanse of water that they would be attempting to cross first thing the next morning, without the benefit of charts, maps, or sextant, in a slim milkweed husk of a *mishoon* that had been stored at the bottom of a pond.

Later that windless night, Squamiset ascended the column of smoke from the fire to the sky world, where he could sometimes achieve a far-reaching view. Tonight's visions were hazy and wavering, distorted by smoke and heat vapors from the fire. Still, they gladdened him. The extensive shoals protecting their island destination were clearly visible as ragged strips of white in a swirling green ocean. Thick banks of fog rolled in and out, keeping the land hidden at certain moments and giving the islanders a comfortable sense of living in a world unto itself. These people were well nourished, sleek, tall, and sun-bronzed. Their harvests were plentiful: corn, squash, beans, grapes, berries, fish, shell-fish, waterfowl, even the occasional whale. It was possible, perhaps even likely, that Squamiset and the two young men in his charge would not live to experience those plentiful harvests, those surf-washed beaches. Even if not, he was still glad. It did his spirit good to see a group of his people living so well, immersed in their traditions, healthy, and as yet undisturbed by the immense changes that had swept the mainland.

Suddenly he found himself carried backward again into the uncon-ditional, frozen world of memory. Four of those captured by Master Wight in the year of the English God 1602 had died at sea. The rest, including Squamiset, had been sold to a slave merchant in Cádiz. Master Wight must not have received much gold for them, for they were filthy and terrified after that long ocean voyage, pale and sickly and barely able to stand, blinking in the bright Spanish sunlight. They were taken in cages through a strange, arid, sunbaked landscape to a slave market in the city of Málaga. On the first day of this market, his Mannomoyik cousins were sold. He never saw them again. On the second day, Squamiset him-self was sold, purchased by a group of monks. The monks treated him kindly, feeding and clothing him and cutting his hair in their odd, bald-pated style. He lived with them for four months in a monastery among olive groves in a narrow mountain valley. He even began to learn their language. But he couldn't bring himself to love their God as they wished him to. He was sick with longing for his forested home across the sea.

One moonlit night he stole out of the monastery and set off on foot for the coast. With his shaven head and rope-belted habit, the people welcomed and fed him, and he made his way from village to village until he reached the port of Cádiz. There he found a ship, and an English sea captain, speaking broken Spanish, promised to take him to a place called

Virginia in exchange for six months of servitude. Squamiset should have been more suspicious, but he craved the air of his own land, and his craving made him blind. The first night at sea the captain's crew fell upon him, and he found himself chained in the darkness between the decks. They took him to London, where the captain sold him to a wealthy lord with an interest in New World curiosities.

In all, Squamiset spent six years in England. When his hair grew out, the lord who owned him made him dress in fanciful Indian garb and paraded him through the streets of London as a spectacle along with a chained bear and six American raccoons on braided cowhide leashes. Despite these indignities the lord was not a terribly cruel master, and the other servants of the household fed Squamiset well and treated him with grudging respect. The lord owned several large estates, so the household constantly traveled, and Squamiset saw many parts of England. The lord provided him with a tutor, George Robinson, with whose help he was able to master the English tongue.

As the seasons wore on, the prospect of living out his life in this strange land across the ocean plunged him into despair. He longed to hear the voices of those he loved, his mother and father and cousins and friends. He often dreamed of his beautiful young wife. Finally, he struck upon the idea of telling the lord a story. The story featured a hill of gold half a day's walk inland from Mannomoy, his home village. He described the hill in convincing detail: how it was overgrown with trees and ferns; how there was a stream trickling down its southern flanks with tea-colored water and pebbles that glinted in the sun; how if you dug in the soil beside this stream, you would strike a bedrock of solid gold.

It took less than a month for the gentleman to outfit a ship. In the presence of an archbishop of the Church of England and Squamiset's tutor, George Robinson, the lord asked Squamiset to swear allegiance to King James. Squamiset did so with alacrity. He would have sworn allegiance to a pigeon or a cockroach or a sewer rat to get back to his own land. By this time he'd begun to experiment with the practice of leaving his body to travel, but he didn't have the strength to travel across the ocean. Home was just a memory, frozen in the moment he'd left it and faded with the passage of time. He had no inkling of the plagues.

Back at the fire by the estuary, Squamiset took a deep breath, his heart aching as the memory-world faded. The fire was dying. Beside it, his charges sprawled on beds of grass. These two young men sleeping on the ground were the only people Squamiset had to worry about now, and he harbored a growing affection for them. But that didn't keep him from mourning everything and everyone he had lost.

Nine

Squamiset roused the young men before dawn. They provisioned the *mishoon* with smoked clams and water gourds sealed with beeswax, and Squamiset chanted a blessing, crumbling tobacco between his fingers into the wind. They were dragging the *mishoon* down into the reeds when they heard the baying of hounds.

"Get in," Squamiset said. "Make haste." Will leapt into the prow, and Natoncks took the middle. Squamiset pushed them out and took the stern. The reeds whispered over the hull as the *mishoon* nosed its way toward open water.

The eastern sky was lightening as they paddled down the estuary, the air filled with the mossy smell of brackish water and the cleaner, salty tang of the ocean. Soon they came to a channel, and they rode the ebbing current out into a bay ringing with the high-pitched cries of terns. Behind them the baying of hounds had grown louder, now mingling with excited shouting in English. Glancing over his shoulder, Will spotted a pack of mastiff hounds, their noses to the ground as they ran frantically back and forth over the abandoned campsite. Piercing the gloom on the eastern horizon, the red sun glinted on the search party's steel helmets and corselets as the militiamen reached the shore of the estuary.

Heart pounding, he caught Squamiset's eye. The old man nodded pointedly at Will's paddle, and Will tried to keep his focus on sweeping it forcefully through the water. But there was something wrong with his left hand. It seemed to be turning green. His bare feet began to change, too, and his tunic and the sides of the *mishoon*—all turning the same seawater green and winking and dancing with the scattered light reflecting off the bay. He could barely make out Natoncks and Squamiset as they faded into the background of sky and seawater. Will's arms and legs had taken on the color of seawater, as had the *mishoon*. If he squinted it was almost as if he were kneeling in the air just above the wavelets—only it wasn't air, because he could feel the press of the wooden hull on his knees and the steady resistance of his cedar paddle as it swept through the water.

"Ho, Toyusk." Natoncks had taken to calling Will by his old childhood nickname.

"Ho, Natoncks. Are you still there?"

"Paddle on, Will," came Squamiset's calm voice. "This illusion will not last long. It is better if the soldiers don't see which direction we are taking."

Will adjusted his grip on the smoothly hewn handle and dug in. The roar of the breakers at the entrance to the bay heightened his anxiety. He wished he were a stronger swimmer.

The tide sucked the *mishoon* through a gap in the beach, and the ocean opened out before them like an endless reflection of the sky. Beyond the breakers the surface was surprisingly calm, gently heaving swells of green seawater gleaming and rose-tinged in the limpid dawn light. Will dragged the green-tinged paddle through the translucent seawater. "Ease up," Squamiset suggested. "Keep your strokes quick and light, as if you are merely caressing the sea."

Will nodded. Behind them the mainland was receding at a reassuring rate. There was no longer any sign of their pursuers, but ahead of them the empty ocean loomed. On that immense expanse of water the *mishoon* was no more than a frail sliver.

Soon Squamiset's illusion faded, and everything took on a reassuringly solid state. Will's hands were cramped from holding the paddle, and his kneecaps ached from kneeling on the smooth wooden hull. A grey-winged gull harassed the men in the *mishoon*, circling and mewling like a kitten. In the last few moments it had become emboldened, gliding along a few yards above Will's shoulder, cocking its head to peer down at him with a calculating yellow eye. It flapped in to perch on the prow, clearly interested in the smoked clams, which were concealed in seaweed behind Will's feet. He tried to sweep it off with his paddle, but the gull merely spread its wings and floated up into the wind for a moment; then it reclaimed its perch with an irritable squawk. Its gaze was avid, scornful. A bloodred fleck decorated the tip of its dangerous-looking beak.

"Is this one of your Manitoo, Squamiset?"

"Perhaps. But it is probably no more than a scavenging gull."

"I suppose your Manitoo are *noble* creatures, not pestilential thieves such as this." As if it had comprehended Will's insult, the gull stuck out its neck and screeched with resentful aggression. Will swiped at it again with the paddle. The gull dodged easily, hanging suspended in the wind as if by an invisible string, and then re-alighted on the prow.

"Toyusk . . . " Natoncks said Will's nickname reprovingly, shaking his head with amusement.

Squamiset asked, "Have you ever watched a gull fly in a storm, Will? It is a spectacle of beauty."

"I have not." Will resumed his paddling. He would grant that the bird had some pretty features: the muscular power in its satin-grey wings, its vivid snow-white breast, a splash of black velvet on its tail. It did appear quite at home on the open ocean, which was more than Will could say for himself. As far as he was concerned, however, a gull was still a pest. *Sea rats* his brother Zeke called them.

The thought of Zeke made him homesick. Somewhere out on this endless ocean, far to the south, Zeke might be gazing out at a similar vastness from the deck of his merchant schooner. Will dearly wished that they could talk to each other across those incalculable miles. He was eager to tell his own version of the events in New Meadow before Zeke heard the official version.

To pass the hours, alternating English with Algonkian to include both Will and Natoncks, Squamiset recounted his long exile in England. In London, he said, the lord who was his master had allowed him a measure of freedom to explore, though he was constantly accompanied by other household servants to ensure that the lord's valuable possession would not run away. "Off and on, for a time, I was distracted from my woes. London is a strange and fascinating place. Do you know it, Will?"

Will shook his head. "I visited once as a child with my mother, but I was too young to remember. I can scarcely remember Devonshire, and we lived there until I was seven." Squamiset nodded. His gaze turned inward, toward the distant past.

"There was much to see in London, and much to learn. As I think I mentioned, the lord provided me with a tutor, George Robinson. He was a good lad, and it was with his help that I became proficient in your language. The lord was pleased with my progress. As a reward, he allowed me to accompany him to theatrical plays. These I enjoyed greatly, especially the ones put on by the King's Men. You know the great William Shakespeare?"

Will laughed delightedly. "Of course I do. It fills me with wonder to think that you saw plays by him. And that I should be learning it here, in this tiny canoe in the middle of the ocean, with a pair of, with a pair of . . . " he trailed off, shaking his head.

"With a pair of savages?" The old man did not smile, but the look in his eyes was wry and kind.

"I'm sorry. It's just that I'm so accustomed to the word. My people use it, that is, most of them—"

The old man held up his hand. "The fault is not yours, Will; there is no need to apologize. Words are powerful, but they are only words. And English is a language with lies built in; one can't truly master it unless he knows how to use them. But the sooner you learn our *Massachusett* tongue, the easier it will be for you to speak the kind of truth that Natoncks can understand."

Will glanced at the young Misquinnipack, who gazed back at him with a friendly and questioning demeanor.

"All the time I was in England," Squamiset continued, "I applied myself to learning your language. After seven years, I became a good enough liar to arrange a ship that would carry me home. The ship's master was a fat Englishman, jolly and red-cheeked, with great white whiskers that gave him the appearance of an overfed otter. He found me amusing, and believed my story about the mountain of gold. But I knew his goodwill would evaporate when he discovered it was all a lie. So I kept retelling the story."

"'You will find it just as I described it,' I told him. 'From a distance, it looks like any other low mountain covered in forest, with a few outcroppings of yellow stone at the top. We shall follow a streambed to the summit, and I will show you where you can scrape the dirt with your fingernails to reveal the gold bedrock beneath.' It was a necessary lie, Will. Do you understand?"

"Fully. Please go on."

"We set sail at the beginning of March in the year of your God 1609. The night before boarding the ship, I sat under a full moon on the breakwater in Plymouth Port. There I had my most important vision, that of the osprey Manitoo that was to become my counselor and protector. This Manitoo promised I would reach my home country alive. I offered my entire supply of tobacco in gratitude. I had been in exile for seven years.

"On the crossing, I paced the ship. I slept out on the deck beneath the stars, no longer able to tolerate walls or ceilings. The voyage wore on, and the ship drew closer. The day came when I could smell the pines of my country on the breeze. I rejoiced in silence, scarcely able to contain my excitement.

"One day, just after sunup, the lookout shouted, 'Land!' I glimpsed it in the mate's spyglass: a hazy line of low forest, golden-red in the first light of sunrise. I waited for the ship to draw closer. Our progress was slow. The breeze was fitful, and the sails could not be kept taut. When we finally came to within a bowshot of shore, I drew in my breath and dove over the rail into the sea. Coming up for air, I heard enraged shouts from the ship, followed by the popping of musket fire. I was not afraid, though, for the Manitoo had told me that it was my destiny to die an old man.

"I swam for shore. I made it to the beach and sprinted for the forest, stripping off my English clothing as I went. I kept only this riding jacket that my tutor George Robinson had given me as a parting gift."

Squamiset held out the tattered lapel of the jacket, which must have been bright scarlet years ago, with silver buttons smartly glittering. Now the few remaining buttons were blackened and dull. "The captain and his crewmen rowed ashore. They brought their hounds to pursue me through the forest, but I knew how to conceal myself, even from dogs. The hounds sniffed and whined and bayed out their frustration, but they could not find me. The captain cursed my name, so disgusted was he that I had lied to gain my freedom. He swore he would search until he found me, and when he found me, he would make me regret that I'd ever been born.

"Feeling the power of the Manitoo rising up within me, I evoked a hideous growling from every direction, like a hundred angry lions. The hounds whimpered, and the frightened Englishmen fled back to the beach. I followed at a distance and watched as they rowed in terror back to the ship.

"The captain was wise enough to see that he'd been beaten. There was no mountain of gold. Even if there were, he would never find it without a guide in what he believed was a dangerous and unforgiving wilderness. He bellowed curses across the water, denouncing me as a traitor, a lying heathen, and a blackhearted Judas. He vowed to make sure that any Englishman visiting this coast would shoot me on sight." Squamiset shook his head with a distant, rueful smile.

"On the next tide, the ship set sail for England. I sat on a rock and feasted upon oysters as I watched it disappear over the horizon. At long last, I was free.

"I ran through the forest, laughing aloud. In my mind I rehearsed what I would say to my mother and father, and to my uncle, the old *powwaw* with whom I'd begun to study before my kidnapping. I thought about my wife, who would no longer be as young as I remembered. I thought about my sons; I was sure I would recognize them, although by then they would have been nearly your age, Will.

"I knew the trails," Squamiset continued, "but the land was strangely overgrown. There were fewer open meadows than I remembered, and there was a deep silence in the forest that seemed odd to me. I assumed it was because I had been so many years away."

Squamiset's expression had become stormy. Natoncks, not understanding the words but sensing the emotion behind them, stared at him with concern. Will found himself wishing the old man would stop talking. The arrival home would make a perfectly happy ending to his story. But with a sinking feeling in his stomach, Will understood that it could not be so.

"What I found when I came to my home village is difficult to describe, Will. All the houses were collapsed and rotting. All the fields were overgrown with brambles. I wandered from place to place, baffled, puzzling over the fate of my people. Had they moved away in search of better hunting grounds? It wasn't unheard of for an entire village to do so, although I thought it strange that my people would leave so suddenly, after so many generations in one place.

"And then, in what had once been the central meeting area of the village, I discovered them. At first I thought it was just a great pile of brush and broken pots and clothing. This was troubling enough, for the waste had always been kept apart from the dwelling places, and my people were too tidy to have left such a mess. Then I noticed something else—something that made me want to close my eyes and run off into the forest and never open them again.

"I didn't run, and I didn't close my eyes. Trembling, I bent down to look. There were familiar shapes among the brambles and broken pottery. Empty-eyed skulls, leg bones, rib cages half-buried in dirt and brush. The bodies must have been picked over by crows and vultures, but bits of dried flesh and hair remained. Some of my people were wrapped in blankets. Their bodies were overgrown with saplings and wild vines of pumpkin and squash."

There was a hollowness in Will's chest. "It grieves me to hear this," he said after a moment.

"As it should, Will. Those who died suffered great pain and sadness. Those who did not die must have fled into the forest in confusion and panic. And it wasn't only my home village. As we saw in the old Nehantic village, many others were wiped out too."

"It was our fault, wasn't it? The English. Did we not bring the plagues?"

Squamiset gave him a curious look. "Many bad things come to pass without anyone to blame, Will. Perhaps the plagues were brought over in the ships of French or Dutch traders long before the English arrived. Or perhaps, as many believe, they were your God's way of clearing the land for his chosen people. If so, he is a cruel god, would you not agree?"

"Yes," Will replied simply.

"In the beginning, even after the plagues, the people of this land stood ready to welcome the English as brothers. When the first of your ships landed, my people came bearing gifts. More often than not, they were greeted by the barrels of muskets. Why do you think that was, Will? I ask you."

Looking out over the heaving sea, Will could think of no logical reason. "I honestly don't know."

"I shall tell you why. Because the English believe that this entire land has been granted them by their God. They do not wish to share it with my people, who have lived upon it since the beginning of time. Englishmen such as Governor Rockingham dread the idea that their religion, which they prize above all else—even gold and property— might get mixed up with ours. Your church allows only one day a week for the Sabbath. For us, every day is the Sabbath. This causes your churchmen to despise us. They do not want their sons and daughters to possess so much freedom, Will. Why else have they pursued you so far? But perhaps these are questions for another time. Shall I continue my story?"

"Please do," Will said, matching his paddling to the rhythm of the other two, lifting it up and dipping it once again into the swells as he listened.

"With my people gone, I became a wanderer. I journeyed south to the Manhates at the edge of the Dutch colonization, and north to the great lake of the Iroquois. Everywhere I went, I witnessed my people losing their faith in the old ways. Traditions were abandoned like broken pottery; ancient rites, unpracticed, were forgotten. We did not understand your religion. It was strange to us that your ancestors had murdered the son of their own God. If Jesus Christ had come down among us, we told ourselves, we would have welcomed him, as we tried to welcome you. But you had guns, steel blades, books of printed words. Many began to believe your God was stronger.

"I wandered north and east to the upper Quinnehtukqut, the village of the Sokokis band by a roaring falls, where I took a second wife. But my visions made me restless, so I wandered south, back through the coastal lands of the Pequot and Narragansett, whose sachim Miantonomo was a prophet of our unification. For years, I wandered from one place to the next, avoiding the expanding English settlements as much as possible. I sought visions and developed my powers of Sight and illusion making. I dreamed of darkness dispelled, of peace returning to my stricken land. I wanted my people to be whole again and to live as one with the land and waters that had always sustained us.

"I returned to the Sokokis on the upper Quinnehtukqut, which was at that time still beyond the reach of English fur traders. I lived there for many years, spending more and more of my time walking alone in the vision worlds. On the coast, I could see that more ships were arriving, each bringing hundreds of Englishmen and women desiring to plant new fields, build new towns, and multiply. English outposts crept northward on the Quinnehtukqut River, and it seemed fated that my adopted Sokokis would be driven out. The world I had known as a child was gone forever. For a time, I was lost in despair.

"Then one night, sitting by a fire, I ascended the column of smoke to the sky world. There I overheard a great council of ancestors discussing ways to heal this afflicted land. It was decided that a journey should be undertaken to Sowwaniu, the home of Cautántowwit, Bringer of Seeds. It was decided that I, though no longer a young man, should be the one to undertake it.

"From that day forward the visions became more intense—and less understandable. I caught glimpses of the journey to Sowwaniu: sun-washed islands under unfamiliar skies; strange, clear, glowing green waters. There was much I did not understand, so I went to a mountaintop to seek clarity. The osprey Manitoo came to me there. It had been many years since I'd seen him, but it was he who sent me to find you, Will. On that mountaintop, the osprey showed me your face."

"And what about Natoncks?" Will asked. The young Musqunnipuck glanced up at the mention of his name, having lost himself in the repetitive rhythm of paddling as Will and Squamiset conversed in English.

Squamiset shook his head. "Natoncks will accompany us on this first leg of the journey only. He shall remain on the island, but we shall have to go much further."

"Much further?"

"Yes, Will. To the southwest. To Sowwaniu, home of the Bringer of Seeds." Squamiset took a moment to explain what he'd been saying to Natoncks. Will was struck by how nonchalantly the Misquinnipack seemed to accept the idea of permanent exile in a place none of them were certain even existed. As for Squamiset's promise about the two of them having to travel further, he supposed it was all the same to him. All he knew is that he could never go home.

They paddled along in silence for a time. The face of the ocean had begun to change. The wind was in their faces now, and dark purple storm clouds thronged the horizon. Will felt a prickling between his shoulder blades. The others seemed to have picked up the cadence of their paddle strokes. Something was wrong. "What is it?" he finally asked.

"Storm coming," Squamiset replied. His expression was tense. Natoncks glanced back at Will and shook his head with companionable solemnity.

Within moments, the sea had transformed. The swells had become pitching hills opaque as green soapstone. The wind shrieked in Will's ears, sending white foam tumbling down the slopes of waves in lacy ribbons. Columns of spray swirled up from the waves like angry ghosts, throwing themselves into the wind to dissipate over the churning surface. Between each huge wave, Will's stomach dropped sickeningly as the *mishoon* plummeted into the trough between the heaving walls of seawater. Will couldn't shake the memory of his mother in her sailcloth envelope, spiraling deeper and deeper into an ocean he remembered as precisely this shade of green. The *mishoon* rocked to and fro, and water poured in over the sides.

Will glanced back wide-eyed.

"Keep paddling!" Squamiset shouted over the wind. "Steady movement will keep us upright!" Natoncks looked tense as he dug his paddle into the churning water. Will concentrated on making his own strokes as strong and steady as he could. The effort to keep the *mishoon* moving became the sole focus of his existence. No other action seemed possible.

The clouds unleashed a bucketing rain, and darkness fell, and Will was sure they were all going to drown. But eventually the wind subsided. The rain ended, and the stars came out. Soaked through and kneeling in cold water up to his thighs, he shivered incessantly. The others had put down their paddles and were using empty water gourds to bail out the *mishoon*. Will had never tried to sleep on his knees, but he did so now. Natoncks showed him how to brace the paddle against the sides of the *mishoon* so that it formed a kind of support over which he could drape himself forward. His whole body ached. In his dreams he was still paddling up and down the swells.

Ten

He awoke with a start. It was day again, and the world was obscured by dense white fog. The wind had died down, and the *mishoon* rolled in a long slow pattern over an undulating sea. Natoncks was bailing with a gourd while Squamiset steered with his paddle to keep them at right angles to the swells. The old man's weathered face was alert—not cheerful but not morose either. Will drew comfort from the sight of it.

The old man gestured with his chin toward the food supplies in the hull. Will leaned over and uncovered a few smoked clams and poured himself a handful of parched corn, washing it down with a swallow of fresh water. He held up the water gourd, which was close to empty. Two more sealed gourds were all that remained. "We shall reach the island today," Squamiset said, peering ahead into the thick fog. "Or we shall not reach it at all."

Will set the gourd back in the hull. A noise that had been in the background since he'd awakened—so constant and unchanging that he hadn't even noticed it—suddenly grew louder in his ears: a dull roar, like an approaching waterfall. "What's that?"

Natoncks stopped bailing. He glanced at Squamiset, tilting his head as if he too was listening. "A meeting of waters," the old man said, sitting back on his heels. "A tidal boundary, a place where the sound joins the deeper water of the open ocean. We must cross over it. I believe we are close to the island."

The noise grew louder. It sounded like a white-water rapid. "When you are ready." The old man gestured toward the paddle on Will's knees. Natoncks had already started paddling.

The hull of the *mishoon* knifed through the water toward the roaring shoal. Through the fog, Will could make out a wall of standing waves, like a rain-swollen river in the middle of the ocean. There was no beginning and no end to it—and no way to get around it. Will mouthed a prayer to God. Just in case, he added a few improvised words for the Manitoo as well. He gritted his teeth and concentrated on keeping up the same quick cadence as the other two, and the *mishoon* collided with the torrent. The standing waves were even bigger than they'd looked, as big as houses, with chasms of churning white water between them. The thundering water was so loud that no other sound was possible.

When they struck the current, the prow lurched to one side. Will lost his balance and released one hand from the paddle to steady himself on the rim of the *mishoon*, which rocked sickeningly. Squamiset yelled to him to keep paddling—it was the first time Will had ever known him to raise his voice—and Will grasped the handle and plunged the paddle into the raging white water. The *mishoon* tilted into the current, almost capsizing, then compensated by tilting against the current. Seawater poured into the hull like a clear green millstream over a dam. The three fugitives had one second to look at each other in wide-eyed shock before they were plunged bodily into the fast-moving current.

Will gasped for breath and fought to the surface as the cold water lifted him up to the crest of a standing wave. He caught a glimpse of the sun through swirling fog before the current hurtled him down into a trough. He fought to keep his head above water, but the current inevitably dragged him under. Beneath the surface, everything was strangely peaceful. He kicked his legs and windmilled his arms, trying to fight his way back to the surface, but the current pulled him down with too much force. He'd nearly run out of air when a pale, blurred figure frog-stroked toward him from the depths. The figure looked familiar, and then he recognized his mother's face from his visions, pale and watery green, long green-blonde hair swirling about her smiling lips. His throat ached. As he opened his mouth to greet her, his lungs filled with seawater.

Her powerful arms embraced him. The rushing green faded slowly to midnight black, and he knew he was losing consciousness. His last thought was how strong his mother had become, swimming around all these years under the sea.

Will awoke vomiting seawater on a bright sand beach. Squamiset knelt astride him, using both hands to pump his chest. Natoncks, beside him, saw that Will was alive and sat back on his heels in relief. After much gasping, coughing, and hiccuping, Will was able to sit up. Salt water streamed from his nostrils, and his lungs burned, but he was alive. Looking around, he saw that they were at the tip of a long peninsula of sand. The fog had burned off, but the sand was still cool to the touch. Squamiset offered him a drink from one of the sealed gourds he'd managed to recover from the *mishoon*. "Thank you," he said hoarsely. "And you, Natoncks." Natoncks inclined his head.

They rested awhile on the beach. As he recovered, Will reveled in the sugary white sand between his toes, the solidity of dry land, the cloudless blue sky, and the absence of pitching and swaying. A light breeze made the dune grass whisper, and in the distance they could hear the cackle of gulls. Otherwise, the sand point was steeped in silence. They set off toward low hills visible as a faint green haze to the south. The dry sand was soft, making walking arduous. In some ways this beach wasn't all that different from several they'd crossed on the mainland, but there was something unmistakably foreign in the air. It was as if they were walking through a dream—as if they'd arrived not just on an island but on an entirely new continent.

They trudged through a dwarf forest of windswept pine and along the edge of a tidal pond with a narrow opening to the sea. Millions of tiny orange crabs scuttled away in the dune grass, their armored carapaces clicking noisily like a miniature army in retreat. An osprey circled above their heads, its snow-white breast and mottled underwings vivid in the morning light. "Is that yours?" Will asked.

"No." Squamiset shook his head. "But observe how fat it is. With luck, we too shall become well-fed and sleek." The land widened to a point where the peninsula joined the island, and the concentration of shore life increased. Flocks of gulls and terns plied the waters beyond a fringe of gentle surf. Black-and-white oystercatchers with powerful orange beaks plucked at the sand while plovers and turnstones sprinted to pluck morsels from the retreating waves as new breakers crashed in. The shiny black heads of seals bobbed on the swells. The fresh breeze was laden with the smell of feeding fish whose slicks tamed the water in long ribboning strips a few hundred yards offshore.

The breeze was welcome, for the sun was starting to get hot, and there was no shade. The drinking gourd long since empty, Will wondered where a person might find fresh water on an island where the ground seemed to consist entirely of sand. He was about to query Squamiset on this problem when a long heavy object thrummed into the sand at his feet and he jumped back with a yelp. Natoncks dropped into a reflexive crouch, and Squamiset, apparently unfazed, bent to examine the object sticking out of the sand. It was a throwing spear, fashioned from some limber wood decorated with runelike carvings, whittled to a narrow taper at the end and still vibrating ominously from the impact. Squamiset dropped to his knees, bowing his head as if in supplication. Natoncks followed suit, and Will, with reluctance, did the same.

Three islanders strode up, the skin of their arms and faces sunbronzed and glistening with oil. Two carried bows, and there was no doubt in Will's mind that these tall hunters could have their arrows nocked and loosed in the blink of an eye. The third man—the spearman—was empty-handed. He was six inches shorter than his companions, with gold hoops in his ears and a badly pockmarked face. One of his eye sockets held only a shiny scar where the eye should have been. His attitude conveyed a sense of violence that made Will's scalp prickle. This man jerked his weapon out of the sand and pointed it at the center of Will's chest. Will opened his hands to show that he was no threat. The one-eyed islander scowled and pressed the spearpoint—a long, sharp, flaked leaf of obsidian—against Will's breastbone. Natoncks moved to grab hold of the spear, but Squamiset caught his arm. "Do not be afraid," the old man said to Will. "This man will not harm you."

Will gave him a worried sideways glance. The spearman's tattooed arms were muscular, and the razor-sharp obsidian blade pressed a pinpoint ache at the center of his chest. It would only take another inch of thrust to pierce his heart. The islander spat out an incomprehensible Algonkian phrase, the angry glare of his single eye not leaving Will's face. He wore a wampum neckband in a checkerboard pattern, and his hair was pulled to one side and wrapped with red and black string like the forelock of a cosseted horse. "What did he say?" Will asked, not daring to look away.

"That you have the features of a parson," Squamiset replied. "He has met one before—on the mainland, I suppose—and the memory is not a pleasant one for him."

"Tell him I'm no parson. I'm not even a good Christian."

Squamiset spoke in reassuring tones, gesturing over his shoulder toward the sand point; Will assumed he was recounting the events that had brought them here. Natoncks nodded periodically, and the hard expressions of the two taller Indians, younger men than they had first appeared, gradually began to soften. But the one-eyed islander didn't lower his spear. When Squamiset finished, the spearman released a torrent of angry, guttural speech.

"What does he say now?" Will asked, staring into the single blazing eye. Squamiset and Natoncks had gotten to their feet, but Will was forced to remain on his knees, the spear tip still pressing into the center of his chest.

"He believes you bring death to this island. He says that if you do not go away voluntarily, he will be forced to kill you."

"Tell him I have no way to leave at the moment. Otherwise, I would gladly go."

"Don't worry, Will. I'll persuade him." Squamiset spoke again, his voice louder than before, though still calm. The spearman replied at length, his words low-pitched and venomous. The single, hate-filled eye never left Will's face, and the spearpoint continued to nudge painfully against Will's sternum.

Eventually, something the old man said convinced the islander to lower his spear. Will got up, brushing the sand off his knees. One of the tall bowmen, who was just Will's age or a little older, caught his eye and nodded solemnly. Will nodded back. The crisis seemed over. But then the one-eyed man tossed the spear into the air and caught it just below the point. In a single, fluid movement he stepped forward, gripped Will's left wrist, and drew the blade across his forearm.

Will cried out. A beaded line of scarlet sprang into the incision, followed by a stinging pain. The spearman stepped back, muttering something under his breath, and turned to stride away across the sand. The two young islanders stood looking elsewhere, as if embarrassed. Squamiset watched the spearman walk away, shaking his head regretfully. "Why the devil did he do *that*?" Will asked, holding his arm.

Squamiset pulled a handful of damp moss from one of his pouches and handed it to Will to stanch the bleeding. Will took it, staring angrily after the retreating spearman. "He wanted these young men to see that an Englishman can bleed," Squamiset replied.

"I could have told them that."

"He will leave you in peace now. He's made his point."

"It would have been better not to come," Will said bitterly. "We should have gone west instead, into the wilderness. Or directly southwest, if you prefer, to search for the home of your precious seed bringer." The wound on his forearm was superficial, but it stung. The greater wound, of course, was to his pride. He regretted that he'd been unable to react more quickly to deflect the spear or at least to offer some measure of resistance.

Natoncks gave Will a sympathetic look. They set off with the two young hunters toward the main body of the island. Will began to feel better as they strolled through a small oak forest punctuated by low-lying, mossy dells. Beyond this forest the main part of the island consisted of a rolling, treeless heath that reminded him of the Devonshire moors he'd wandered as a child. The Atlantic Ocean glittered on the horizon, and the light had a hazy, liquid quality that he found very beautiful.

The young men led the visitors to their summer village, which they called Wannasquam. It consisted of around three-dozen houses clustered at the edge of a freshwater pond that was sheltered by high dunes. Unlike the bark-covered *wetuwash* of the Misquinnipack, the islanders' houses were sheathed in mats of woven reeds. Lush vegetable gardens surrounded many of the houses, and bean vines spiraled up around cornstalks that rose from a carpet of broad squash leaves. Beyond the dunes was the open Atlantic. Breaking surf provided a pleasant background noise. The breeze smelled of wild roses and salt spray.

In one of the gardens a gang of children lolled on a platform made of saplings and stared down at the newcomers with wide-eyed curiosity. A tough-looking girl of around ten or eleven with a domesticated falcon perching on her shoulder made a sharp-tongued remark that yielded a chorus of high-pitched laughter. A small crowd gathered in the center of the village. On the whole, Will thought, the islanders were a remarkably handsome lot: lean, tall, fine-featured. A straight-backed old man with wispy white braids and bronze bands around his biceps came out to greet Squamiset. They held each other's forearms silently for a long moment, tears glinting in both sets of eyes. Will guessed the old islander was Squamiset's long-lost cousin.

A woman with a silver braid down to her waist came over to look at the cut on Will's forearm. She beckoned him into one of the *wetus*, motioned him to sit on the floor, and ducked out through the sealskin door flap. Alone in the dark, Will looked up at the dome of bent saplings covered in reed mats. The mats were densely woven, though a ray of daylight streamed in through a rectangular gap that had been left in the middle of the ceiling. It felt strange to be sitting in such a place, and for the first time since he'd left New Meadow, Will experienced a twinge of homesickness. He didn't miss Overlock, but he did miss his brother, Zeke, and he missed the hearth and parlor of his own home—even the cramped berth that had been his sleeping place since the age of seven.

The silver-haired woman returned with a bowl of cool pond water and more dried moss. She cleaned the cut and pressed the moss into it. It stung for a moment, but Will could see that it was not a serious wound. She wrapped it with a bandage of pounded reed fiber and motioned for Will to go. He thanked her in his rudimentary Algonkian. She nodded solemnly and squeezed his hand, a gesture so unexpected that he was surprised to find his eyes swimming with tears. He couldn't remember the last time he'd been treated with such kindness by a woman since his mother had died. The women of New Meadow either had children of their own or were too proper to give their affection to a solitary orphan like Will.

That evening the islanders lit a bonfire in the dunes. They laid out a welcoming feast of shellfish and lobster on reed mats, but for some reason Will had no appetite. A pretty girl around his own age gestured toward one of the mats and gave him an encouraging smile, causing his heart to leap. He took a small lobster—a meal he normally would have devoured with pleasure—but tonight he could only pick at it.

After the meal, he felt strange. There was drumming and singing and later a dance, a dizzying blur of shell earrings and wampum collars glinting in the firelight. Squamiset was surrounded by admirers, and Natoncks seemed already to have made friends with some of the young islanders, including the pretty girl who had smiled at Will and the two bow hunters whom they'd first encountered. But Will had no energy for trying to communicate in a language he barely spoke, and he sat in the shadows hugging his knees. The flames seemed to throb in time with the drumbeats. Feeling chilly, he inched a little closer to the fire.

The one-eyed spearman appeared before him. He tossed a driftwood log on the flames, giving Will a strangely suggestive glance as he did so. Will shivered. The flames rose and crackled, shooting sparks high into the starry sky. Will's teeth began to chatter. For all its blazing height, the fire didn't seem to be giving off much warmth.

The healer-woman with the long silver hair came over to look at the dressing on his arm. She pressed her cool hand to his neck and nodded slowly. A moment later she came back with Natoncks and one of the young hunters who wore shell hoops in his ears and pounded copper bands around his upper arms. "Sick, Toyusk?" Natoncks asked, full of polite concern.

"No, I'm fine," Will replied, but the truth was that he didn't feel fine. The night had become a blurred jumble of firelight and dancing shadows, and his teeth were chattering uncontrollably. They led him back to the *wetu*, where the woman indicated that he was to lie upon a sleeping platform. They covered him in layers of heavy sealskin, and Natoncks built a fire in the center of the earthen floor.

The healer returned with a gourd of warm water steeped with herbs and pine needles. The taste was pleasant. Kneeling next to him, she insisted he drink it all. When he was done, she raised her brows and pointed to a large pottery bowl she had set on the floor beside the sleeping platform. All at once an ugly pressure surged up from deep in his gullet. Casting off the skins, he sat and leaned over to vomit in the bowl. The healer nodded with satisfaction, took the bowl out, and brought it back clean. She left it on the floor beside him and tilted her head sideways on pressed-together hands to indicate that Will should sleep.

He lay shivering under the skins, staring up at the smoke flying out through the square hole in the domed roof. He recognized the Pleiades wavering in the sky above the opening. Outside, the drumming went on, now joined by a rising chorus of quavering song that sounded like wolves or the howling of the wind, and the surf pounded out an endlessly varying rhythm in the background. Will felt lonely and inconsolably sad.

Eleven

In the night his condition worsened. His teeth chattered; his bones ached. One moment he was freezing; the next he was on fire. He forgot where he was and called out for Overlock to assist him. Then he began to hallucinate. He saw his brother, Zeke, standing on the deck of his ship, illuminated by the reflection of a dancing, strangely luminescent green sea. He saw a tall frigate sailing into a glassy harbor. There was a cloaked man standing in the prow. His head was blacked out, as if a hole had been torn out of the day.

When he awoke, the sun streamed in through the square opening in the roof. Squamiset sat cross-legged on the floor. "Am I dying?" Will asked.

The old man gazed at him evenly. "It is possible." Squamiset then began to ask a question, but before Will could hear what it was he was lost in the sickening whirl of delirium. He looked at his reflection in a mirror, but something hit the mirror and caused it to shatter. He could see fragment of himself in the shards, but the shards became feathers, and a howling wind blew them away. He was left standing alone on a surface of polished grey stone that stretched away into an infinite horizon of nothingness.

Later still he found himself back in the healer's hut, coughing, because the air was choked with white smoke. Squamiset was there, but he was different. He'd painted a strip of black across his nose and eyes, and his chin and forehead were bone white. Sitting beside him on the floor was the one-eyed spearman. Noticing him, Will groaned. The spearman's pockmarked face was also white with a skull-like circle of black taking up his empty eye socket and crimson all around his mouth, as if he'd been feasting on bloody flesh. Squamiset spoke, but his voice was distorted and incomprehensible. Will opened his mouth to cry out for help, but his words were drowned by a sudden chorus of protesting voices, none of them human, so loud that they shook the smoky air. Will shuddered and closed his eyes. For once he was grateful to escape into delirium.

When he awoke, the silver-haired healing woman knelt beside him. Her eyes were hazel, wise and sad and overflowing with kindness. Seeing that he was conscious, she peeled back the sealskins and rubbed a cool ointment on his chest. Her fingertips were strong yet gentle. Afterward, she held a drinking gourd to his lips. The lukewarm contents were foul, tasting of seawater and rotting fish and a blend of fermented lemon and spicy mustard. He gagged, rolling over to vomit into the bowl she'd placed on the floor. She motioned for him to take another drink. When he refused, she pinched his arm and gave him a stern look. Reluctantly, he forced himself to gulp down a little more of the foul potion. He felt like vomiting again, but this time he managed not to.

Days passed; he had no idea how many. Sometimes when he was awake, the smoke hole was a square of black velvet pricked with stars. Other times the sky was brilliant blue, but most often it was dull white, a swirling void of fog. Sometimes the healing woman was present, standing over him or sitting cross-legged on the floor by a crackling fire. Her face was pleasant to look upon, sun-browned and handsomely wrinkled like the shell of a walnut. He thought she must have been very beautiful as a young woman. Occasionally his imagination seemed to mold itself to this thought, because the woman actually grew younger before his eyes. In those moments her wrinkled cheeks became smooth and girlish, and her hair was not coarse silver but mahogany, tied back in a long braid with silken wisps escaping from it that were backlit auburn in the firelight. The eyes were always the same: wise and sad and overflowing with kindness.

Gradually, he began to recover his appetite. The healer allowed him only liquids: clam broth, fresh water, and several different herb concoctions, most of them unpleasant. When he was able to sit up, Squamiset returned for a visit. "It is good that you are recovering, Will. For a time, your chances didn't look so good."

Will clasped his hands behind his head to stretch his weakened arms. "The healing woman saved me. Without her, I would have died for certain."

"Her name is Mishannock, should you wish to thank her."

"I will find a way to do so." Will paused. "And I believe I owe you a debt of gratitude also. You and the one-eyed islander. He is a *powwaw*?"

Squamiset nodded. "His name is Askooke. His powers are strong because of his association with a black snake Manitoo."

"Is Mishannock one too? A *powwaw*?"

"No. Her knowledge of healing is vast, but she is not a *powwaw*."

"But she is a shape-shifter, no? Sometimes she seems to occupy the form of a much younger woman."

Squamiset produced a rare smile. "That is her granddaughter, Will: Shambisqua. There is a strong family resemblance. I can see how you might have confused them."

After two weeks, Will could walk along the shore of the pond and then across the dunes to the windswept beach. His body was weak, and he had the strong feeling that his previous self—Will Poole, gentleman's son, rebellious youth, aspiring hunter, dreamer, renegade, fugitive, and accidental adventurer—belonged only to the past now, as a series of fading dreams. He felt empty inside, like a bottle whose contents had been poured out onto the dry sand.

• • •

With Natoncks's help, Squamiset had built a *wetu* using bent saplings covered with reed mats plucked and woven from the island's extensive marshes. They'd situated this dwelling some distance from the village in a sunny hollow enclosed on three sides by dunes. It was too late in the summer to plant, but this was no cause for worry. When winter came, Squamiset knew, the islanders would be happy to share.

It was Neepunakeewush, the midsummer moon, and all was as he had foreseen. Eels were running in the tidal streams. Herbs, berries, and groundnuts were in plentiful supply. Apart from the treacherous shoals that protected the island and its distance from the mainland, another natural feature worked to conceal it: the dense banks of fog rolling in from the cooler waters to the south. According to Squamiset's cousin, whose name was Wequashim, Will was one of the few Englishmen ever to have blundered ashore. The others had not lived to tell stories about it. The island was blessed in other ways as well. Moderating breezes from the great southern current made the summers cooler here than on the mainland and the winters milder, meaning that the growing season lasted up to two months longer. Seasonal changes brought in tremendous schools of fish, and seabirds gathered in shrieking flocks to feed upon them. The Manitoo were strong here. Squamiset was aware of them at every moment.

During the long weeks of Will's sickness, Squamiset and Natoncks would bathe in the surf as joyful terns flitted and wheeled above them, filling the air with their piercing cries. They spent the days and evenings mending nets and cordage, harvesting quahogs and oysters, or helping the islanders chase eels into their mazelike weirs. For Natoncks there were ball games and footraces, while Squamiset sat with the elders playing wagering games with shark's teeth or chits of dried fish vertebrae. After dark he would sit beside the fire in Wequashim's *wetu*, talking about the old days in Mannomoy and the people they had loved.

The breakers beat out an unending rhythm on the sand. The tides rose and receded, as did the moon and the sun. Natoncks was safe, and it seemed unlikely that the English search parties would follow them here. Already, Squamiset could feel the goodness of this life lulling him into complacency. How easy it would be to live out his remaining seasons here, well fed and content in the company of new friends and old relations. The years had given him wisdom enough not to hurry through a time of happiness. And yet, deep in his heart, he knew it couldn't last. Eventually, he and Will would be forced to confront their destiny.

There were a few things Will missed about his life in New Meadow. His brother, Zeke. Books and writing materials. Butter. Table salt. East India pepper. Good English apples. On the other hand, life on the island was more pleasant than anything he'd ever known. He possessed the freedom to come and go as he pleased. He could think and say whatever he wished of religion or God or the Indian spirits without worrying about anyone condemning him to the fires of eternal damnation. He could lie on the sun-warmed sand if that was what he wished or spend an entire solitary day whittling or rambling without provoking the slightest concern. The people of Wannasquam were unstintingly generous, giving away the most precious of their possessions upon the slightest provocation. They didn't think twice about sharing their food and drink with him, and, once he recovered, he threw himself into their occupations of hunting, foraging, and harvesting. Will admired their quiet grace, their dry humor, and the way they actually *listened* to each other instead of merely waiting for their turn to speak.

After a month had passed he could handle a *mishoon* tolerably well on his own, though he remained frustrated by his lack of skill in other areas. The young men who had grown up on the island could pluck quahogs from the bottom of an estuary with their toes. They could plunge a spear into the murky brine and lift a flounder the size of a trencher flapping on the point. They could dive to the rocky seafloor and come up with a claw-clacking lobster in each upraised hand. Natoncks had similar skills, but Will was hard-pressed to see anything under water, much less hold his breath long enough to catch a lobster. The closest he came was one rainy afternoon when he emerged gasping with the claw of a small lobster clamped to his index finger. This achievement was the source of hilarity for those in his foraging party, who explained with comical gestures that the man was supposed to catch the lobster, not the other way around.

More frustrating still was the trouble he was having mastering Squamiset's teachings in the field of illusion making. The lessons had begun with basic conjuring tricks. The old man raised an empty clam-shell on the beach, making it click together and say a few simple words in Algonkian. "Now *you* try," he instructed.

Will was at a loss. "But how?"

"Banish all thought. Call on the Manitoo of this island for help."

Will stared at the shell, willing it to move. Nothing. He concentrated so hard that he gave himself a headache, but to no avail. "Maybe I don't have the gift after all," he said.

"But you *do*, Will. You need only cultivate it within yourself."

The next time, Squamiset tried something simpler: he made a strand of dried seaweed blow across a windless beach. Even this basic illusion was beyond Will's capacity. He couldn't make himself believe he had the power to do such a thing, and the truth was, he failed to see the point in trying to develop it. What good would it do him or anyone else to make clams talk or move seaweed across the sand? He saw that his lack of progress was frustrating for his old friend, but there was nothing he could do about it. He couldn't be expected to call upon the Manitoo when he wasn't even sure they existed.

Twelve

One cool morning in September, the month the islanders called Changing Wind, word spread through the village that a whale had beached itself on the southern shore. This was considered a gift from the Manitoo, not only for the meat and blubber and bones but also, depending on the type of whale, for the teeth or the strong flexible baleen, which was of use in tools and personal decoration. By the time the butchering party arrived, the animal was dead, barnacles lining the long jaw, the colossal black body shiny and slightly flattened by gravity as it lay in the surf. Someone handed Will a chert cobble that was round on one side and flaked to a sharp blade on the other.

The smell was staggering as the party began to cut away at the blubber. The skin was tough and difficult to hack through. It was slick with blood and whale oil, and within the first few moments Will's hand slipped. The edge of the cobble sliced deep into the base of his left thumb; he caught a glimpse of white bone before the blood came seeping out to mix with the whale's. The man who had handed him the butchering tool shook his head in exasperation and gave him a piece of blubber, indicating with gestures that Will should keep it pressed to his wounded hand and go back to the village to see the healer. Feeling ashamed, he trudged home over the heathlands.

The healer's hut stood in a meadow at the edge of the freshwater pond. The healer was away gathering herbs, but her beautiful granddaughter, Shambisqua, sat on her heels before the hut shucking quahogs into a woven basket. She had clear honey-colored skin, slightly crooked teeth, and, tied in a loose braid, silken mahogany hair with auburn highlights. As Will approached, she wiped her wrist across her forehead and glanced up. When she saw that he was holding his hand and his forearm was stained with fresh blood, she stood, motioning for him to remove the blubber. The bleeding had slowed enough to reveal the outlines of the wound: a deep gash about two inches long at the base of the thumb crossing over to the heel of the hand. Glancing at it, Will felt an involuntary wave of dizziness. She motioned for him to follow her into the hut. He sat on the sleeping platform with his injured hand raised while she ducked out through the entryway, presumably to fetch some water. The saplings of the *wetu's* framework were hung with bundles of drying herbs and roots. Sunlight slanted in through the smoke hole, painting a bright yellow trapezoid on the earthen floor.

Shambisqua returned with a bowl of water, bringing with her the scent of wild roses and fresh ocean breezes. She motioned for Will to sit on the ground and then sat cross-legged in front of him so that their knees were almost touching. The sudden intimacy of the moment nearly overwhelmed him; he'd never been knee to knee with such a stunningly beautiful girl. She was perhaps a year older than him, but her expertise made her appear much older—a young woman already—while he felt he was still a boy—lanky, awkward, and foreign. Silently, he exhorted himself to retain his dignity, not to slouch or make faces or do anything that would make her think less of him. She reached into a basket for a handful of moss, dipped it in the bowl, and set about cleaning the wound. This smarted, but he remained carefully immobile. He concentrated on the firm pressure of her grip on his wrist and on observing her methodical skill as she worked. But he couldn't help noticing her sad eyes or the curve of her waist and hips beneath the doeskin tunic.

When the wound was clean, she took a handful of dry moss from the basket and placed it on the seeping gash. "Hold," she said, placing Will's right hand firmly over the moss. He held it, and she bound his hand expertly with strips of pounded bark. She inspected this bandage, turning his hand this way and that, then let go.

"Thank you," he said in his rudimentary Algonkian.

She nodded, suppressing a smile.

In the weeks leading up to the corn harvest the women and girls congregated outside the huts to sew *moccasins* and leggings, prepare meals, and make jewelry out of shells. Sometimes they went down to the ocean to swim. They chose a different beach than that of the men and boys, for most of them were modest, and swimming was done in the nude. For their part, the men had nets and weirs to mend, and there were fowl to be shot and quahogs and lobsters to be hauled up out of the bay. But the great fish migrations of summer had passed, and the great fish migrations of autumn had not yet begun, so the young men spent many hours swimming and playing in the surf and racing their *mishoons* on the tricky waters of the open ocean. The older men, having long ago proved themselves, devoted their idle hours to sitting beneath sun shelters overlooking the ocean, smoking tobacco and pokeweed, and indulging their collective obsession with gambling.

Squamiset was by no means immune. Like most older island men, he was particularly fond of a game called *hubbub*. This was played with a reed tray and five disks made from the dried vertebrae of a large fish. The disks were lightweight and regular, painted black on one side and white on the other. The players pounded the sand around the tray with rhythmic violence, causing the disks to jump and flip, showing white and black and white in rapid succession. To increase this effect, the man whose turn it was whisked his hands back and forth over the disks to create a crosswind while the others pounded the sand and smote themselves on chests and thighs, crying out *hub, hub, hub* in voices that could be heard from a great distance. Five disks all white or all black was a double win. Three of one color and two of another was a single win, and four of one color and one of another meant nothing. As long as a man kept winning, he kept the tray. If he lost, he passed it on to the next player.

Piles of goods changed hands—sealskins and trinkets and wampum and harpoons—and it was not unusual for a player to lose everything he possessed in a single afternoon. This was not an occasion for remorse. The loser knew he would not starve among his own people, and the next day he would have the opportunity to win his possessions back. It was a congenial pastime with the advantage of not requiring Squamiset's full attention so that he could allow his mind and spirit to wander. He was grateful for the chance to enjoy this time on the shores of the glittering ocean.

The tray was passed to him, and he began to sweep his hands rapidly to and fro over the disks while the others shouted and pounded the sand. Yes, he was happy. And yet, he was aware that this happiness could not last.

Four white disks and a single black. He passed the tray to the next man, and the shouting and pounding resumed. Often, at dawn or dusk, he would go away on his own to sit on a lonely bluff overlooking the ocean. He would fill his pipe and search his mind for visions. If he was honest, he had to admit that he did not relish the task that had been given him. He preferred to put it off.

The tray came around again. He raised it to his chin and blew on the disks for luck, winking at white-haired Wequashim who sat across the circle from him. He set the tray down on the sand for the pounding and the sweeping. The air shook with his companions' exuberant shouts.

Five black bones. His fortune was very good. Every man had to hand him a piece of dried reed, each piece representing some valuable object that the man had tendered.

Suddenly a chill came over him, like a fast-moving storm cloud covering the sun. He stood, overturning the tray into the sand. The circled players stared up at him in concerned silence. Though *hubbub* was played in good humor, it was at root a serious game and not customarily interrupted.

A white dog that had lately adopted Squamiset and followed him everywhere looked up from its resting place and raised its ears, letting out a thin, unsettled whine. One of the players spoke to him angrily, but when Squamiset did not look down at him, Wequashim, older and wiser, put his hand on the man's shoulder. "Leave my cousin in peace."

Squamiset staggered off down the beach in a daze, and the white dog loped after him with the fur on its shoulders bristling. It was a gusty summer afternoon. The wind whipped sand into his face and eyes, but he didn't notice. He was overwhelmed by a sense of foreboding, a sudden realization that everything was on the brink of change.

He headed toward the long peninsula of sand that the islanders called Nauma, upon which he and Will had first made landfall. He carried no food or water, but it didn't matter. After a long walk, much of it bent forward into a steady north wind, he came to the point of the sand spit and took shelter between two high dunes. He lay on his back, gazing up at the sky.

He remained there for two days. The white dog passed the time sleeping, sometimes getting up to pace the beach. It drank from a small puddle of rainwater in the shell of a broken *mishoon*. It killed a clumsy juvenile seagull and fed upon the carcass of a seal. On the afternoon of the second day a dense fog rolled in, enveloping the old man in cloud. He lay upon the dry sand beneath a ceiling of white nothingness, empty and infinite. In the background he could hear the sounds of the ocean: the screams of gulls and terns, the restive slap of waves, the murmur of shifting tides. The osprey flew out of the fog and flapped in to perch on a piece of driftwood. The dog raised its ears and whined softly.

Squamiset sat up, hugging his knees. "I wondered if you would find your way here."

Like you, old man, I have relations on this island.

"Indeed. I suppose you also have a message for me."

The bird cocked its head and looked him up and down with its scornful yellow eye. *Simple happiness is not enough? You long for a mountain of gold, perhaps? An English paper naming you king of this island?*

"Do not play with me," the old man said ruefully. "You once showed me my destiny, and now that destiny must be fulfilled. Or have you come to tell me otherwise?"

No. You are correct. You must leave this place, and you must take the English boy with you.

"He is a boy no longer, fish hawk. And he has taken a liking to a girl here. It is cruel to force him away."

And yet you must. You know this well enough.

Squamiset nodded. Will wouldn't like it, but there was no point in arguing with a Manitoo. "How soon?" he asked.

Before the snow falls.

"Where are we to go?"

This too you already know. To the southwest. To the home of Cautántowwit, Bringer of Seeds and of the life-giving rains of summer.

"How shall I know when we have gone far enough?"

The bird gazed at him, its flinty yellow eye pitiless. *Do not fret so much, old man. You shall know. Do not doubt it.*

The wind had begun to strip the fog away in tattered shrouds. The osprey spread its wings and soared up into a section of clear sky. It circled higher and higher until it was nothing but a tiny black X in the blue, then a pinpoint; then it was gone.

Thirteen

Everywhere Will turned he saw her face. He went out of his way to walk where he might get a glimpse of her. He said her name just to hear the sound of it on his lips. It was as if he'd caught an illness, a bittersweet malady of the heart that could only be cured by her presence. He whiled away his time, waiting until he had a good excuse to visit the healer's hut. He finally allowed himself to do so on a cool fall morning with a clear blue sky overhead and a bright sun slanting in over the dunes. Mishannock, Shambisqua's slender grandmother, sat on her haunches outside the entryway making bundles from a pile of drying herbs. She got to her feet and held aside the door flap, motioning him in. "Sit," she instructed in Algonkian, indicating a place by the fire beside her grand-daughter, who looked up briefly as he came in but did not meet his eyes.

The old woman unwrapped the dressing and turned his hand back and forth, inspecting the wound thoroughly as Shambisqua tended to the fire. Will tried to relax, surrendering himself to Mishannock's strong, competent fingers. After a moment, he realized that he was holding his breath. He exhaled, and it sounded like a sigh. Shambisqua glanced up at him with an amused expression.

The wound had closed neatly. The healer murmured something to her granddaughter and released his hand. It wasn't new for Will to be ignorant of what was being said. Though he had gained a handle on the rudiments of the language, he could seldom understand when the islanders spoke amongst themselves. He smiled at the old woman. She stared back at him solemnly, her gaze so penetrating that he had to lower his eyes. Shambisqua switched places with her grandmother and gently bathed the wound in fresh water. Once she glanced up, and their eyes briefly met. Afterward, it occurred to him with a pang of embarrassment that he'd been smiling from the moment he entered the hut to the moment he left. Not dignified behavior for a Wampanoag man, but it didn't matter. Shambisqua liked him. Or at least she found him tolerable.

The next night was the autumnal equinox, when darkness and light were evenly matched. The men built a bonfire. The women prepared a *succotash* of corn, squash, and fish in a woven basket filled with heated stones. More stones were brought from the fire to line two *pesuponcks*, sweat lodges, one for the women and one for the men. There was a great deal of singing and dancing to celebrate the harvest, and tobacco was offered to ensure the timely return of *Aukeetamitch*, the moon of spring planting. Will tried not to watch Shambisqua, who sat smiling as another girl spoke into her ear, the two of them wavering prettily in the heat vapors on the far side of the fire. For the occasion of the feast she had put on a wampum neckband and long earrings made of shells. Her hazel eyes sparkled, and, when she smiled, her slightly crooked teeth shone in the firelight. She was luminous, irresistible. A gloomy truth settled over Will like November drizzle: any man on the island could see what he saw. What chance did he have, really?

She sensed his gaze, and their eyes met across the fire. She raised her eyebrows as if to ask if anything were the matter. He shook his head and in the next moment got up to leave. He was in no mood for a feast. How strange and foreign he must appear to her: pale and freckled and clumsy. There were plenty of young men on this island more able and handsome than he. It had been presumptuous of him to imagine himself worthy of more than her friendship. Even that he would have to earn.

. . .

The next morning he knelt on the sand floor of his own hut, break-ing cedar twigs to feed the fire. Natoncks snored under his furs. Squa-miset, as was his wont, had crept out before dawn while the young men were still asleep. Now he returned, ducking in through the door flap followed by the small white village dog that refused to let him out of its sight. The dog leapt up on the far sleeping platform and gave Will a cool, pitying look, as if it had read his innermost thoughts and found them sadly lacking. Squamiset handed Will a bundle of cornhusks that let off wisps of fragrant steam. Will took the food and unwrapped it to reveal a fresh corn cake with tart crane-berries cooked in.

"Mishannock?" he asked.

The old man nodded. The kindhearted healing woman often pro-vided their breakfasts. Squamiset sat cross-legged across the kindled fire and gazed at Will. His craggy face looked longer and older than usual in the firelight. The faded horseman's jacket was stained with maplike coastlines of white salt and had lost the last of its buttons. It was begin-ning to come apart at the sleeves. "Tell me, Will," he said, "have you spoken with the Manitoo of this place?"

Will shook his head. "I believe you when you say they exist, but I've yet to catch a glimpse of one."

The old man was silent for a moment, then got to his feet. He rum-maged around in a basket hanging from the sapling frame of the hut, sat down, and handed Will a small bundle of dried roots. "A powerful herb," he explained. "In English, it is called jimsonweed."

"And what am I to do with it?"

"Crush it and mix it with water. Climb to the highest place you can find and sit still. This herb will smooth a path for you. I'm not certain that you're ready, but we can't wait forever."

Will tucked the bundle inside his hunting shirt and ate some of Mishannock's delicious corn cake. "Shall I do this today?"

"Whenever the inclination takes you."

Finishing the corn cake, Will wiped his hands on his buckskin leggings. Squamiset gazed at him. "We cannot stay here forever, Will. The time approaches when we shall have no choice but to leave." There was a stirring in the shadows, followed by a light groan. Natoncks was awake.

"Do you think it's possible you've misinterpreted the visions?" Will asked. He gestured around the hut, taking in the bundles of drying herbs, the raised sleeping platforms stocked with mats and furs, groggy Natoncks, who had just sat up, and the sharp-eyed white dog. "Do you truly wish to leave all this behind?"

Squamiset shook his head. "I do not wish to leave, Will, but we must. Soon enough, I foresee, the reasons will become apparent to you."

Will made the potion just as the old man had instructed, grinding the root with a mortar and pestle, mixing it with water, and decanting it into a gourd. He didn't necessarily believe that the jimsonweed would allow him to talk to a Manitoo, but he had nothing else to do at the moment, and out of respect for his old friend he was ready to try it.

Not far from the village was a patch of high ground, a hilly expanse with views of the ocean and the rolling moorland. It didn't take him long to find a good spot to sit on a granite boulder at the center of a high knoll. Sitting upon this lonesome stone, he forced himself to drink the potion, which was, as expected, bitter and foul-tasting. Yet it was a pleasant day, mild for autumn, and the moorlands were pretty, undulating yellow-green hills tinged scarlet with the dying leaves of blueberry and huckleberry and other heathland shrubs. The sun burned pale in the milky haze, throwing long shadows across the island. The usual flocks of gulls cried in the distance.

Suddenly he felt ill. Sliding down from the boulder, he retched into the dry grass. And then the sky began to spin. The day grew darker in a progression of awful, shuddering jolts. He rested his forehead against the base of the boulder and lost consciousness.

Some time later he opened his eyes, feeling refreshed and energetic. He had an overwhelming desire to explore. The fog had rolled in, low and swirling, and there was so much about the landscape that he'd never noticed before. The tussocks of dried grass beneath his feet looked like hanks of yellow hair. The twigs of the shrubs, damp from the fog, looked like fingers or claws, black and grasping. Berries dotted the scrub like flecks of scarlet blood. He walked along slowly with his hands behind his back, taking it all in. The fog muffled the cackle of gulls and the distant breakers. He felt as if he were the only person in the world.

And then he heard music. Or perhaps it was only the wind. But it sounded like a reedy, wavering flute tune. The melody was sad and familiar, like something he might have heard in childhood, yet he could put no words to it. He walked in its direction and came to a wall of dense scrub garlanded with thorns. Throwing aside any remaining caution, he plunged headlong into the brambles. The thorns caught at his leggings and tore into the bare skin of his hands and face as he fought his way through.

He emerged into a kind of dell, an oval of widely spaced trees with trunks that curved and spiraled upward like columns of petrified smoke. The ground was humped and springy beneath his feet, the moist earth covered in thick layers of yellow-green moss. Tendrils of fog slipped in and out of the trees. He could no longer hear the music. In the middle of the dell was a small oval pond of tea-colored water cupped in the cushiony yellow moss. A wave of exhaustion overtook him, and he decided to lie down. The moss felt as he imagined a fine feather mattress might feel, only cooler and springier. Above him there was an opening in the trees, swirling white with meandering fog. He closed his eyes.

He dreamed he was a small child with his head cradled in his mother's lap. He gazed up at her face, which was just as he remembered it, radiant and kind, and her auburn hair swayed slowly back and forth as if in a gently alternating breeze. It was more comfortable than anything he could remember. He felt as if he were suspended in a cocoon of boundless security and love.

But then he began to see that there was something wrong. His mother's face had a greenish pallor, and the motion of her hair was strangely repetitive. It was as if her hair were not being blown by the wind at all but as if it were being washed back and forth in a current, like seaweed. And there were fish swimming by. A turtle. A diving duck, snow-white with black on its head and wings, propelling itself with webbed, bright orange webbed feet. Glancing up beyond his mother's face, he could see the surface of the sea shimmering like a liquid mirror.

His mother's hands tightened around his neck, and he couldn't breathe. He knew he should pry her hands off his throat and swim up to the life-sustaining air, but it didn't seem urgent. Perhaps the hands on his neck were not choking him. Perhaps they were helping him to breathe.

Will sat up, blinking. It had been another hallucination, of course, or a vivid daydream brought on by the jimsonweed. Or, perhaps, he supposed—as Squamiset might say—it had been a true vision. In reality he found himself sitting upon a cushion of springy moss beside the small oval pond at the center of the hidden dell. The wavy-trunked trees were also real, spiraling up into the roiling fog. He'd stumbled into an excellent hiding place: the dell wouldn't be visible from the surrounding hills because the trees grew in a low-lying pocket, and their crowns were roughly the same height as the surrounding scrub.

The pond was tea-colored, translucent at the edges and midnight black in the center, where it was impossible to gauge its depth. On the opposite shore was a stand of dried brown reeds. The tops of the reeds began to twitch, and there was a loud rustling. Will got to his feet, heart pounding. He was not alone.

For a moment, nothing happened. Then a duck swam out, black and vivid white with glowing golden eyes. It appeared to be a figment left over from his vision, one of the creatures that had been swimming beneath the sea. It paddled closer, cocking its head so that one incandescent golden eye fixed Will in its gaze. The eye was perfectly round with a small black pinpoint in the center. Will stepped back, alarmed. It was freakish, the bold way this creature beheld him, as if it knew him through and through and would brook no dishonesty or reticence. "Are you a Manitoo?" he asked.

The duck blinked, and suddenly Will could see himself from its perspective, looking up at him from the pond. There were no mirrors on the island; he hadn't noticed that his hair had grown so long. His face was bronzed by the sun and striped with drying blood from the thorns. The duck blinked its strange golden eye again, and Will found himself hurtling through another series of splintered visions. A small round object rolling down to the waterline. Beyond it a tall-masted frigate, ominous and black-hulled, with a tall black-cloaked figure standing at the prow. The decks of the ship blazed into orange flames and disappeared, and Will found himself contemplating an ocean scene of transparent, strangely glowing green water lapping a blindingly white beach. It occurred to him with a surge of terror that he might be glimpsing his own future and therefore, quite possibly, his own demise. "Stop it," he said, pressing his fingers against his eyelids. "I don't want to see any more."

In the next moment he was sprinting across the surface of the pond, lifted by the flapping of strong, well-made wings. Then he was in the air, and it felt natural to be flying, as in his old dreams, and he was soaring up over the tops of the wavy trees and the scarlet-tinged shrubs and up into the swirling fog, a fast-flowing whiteness. He worried that he would lose his bearings because there was nothing to orient by, and yet he seemed to possess a kind of internal compass. He kept climbing higher until he broke through to clear air. He gazed down at the heavy white fog bank that enveloped the island. An immense joy flooded through him. He could feel the heat of the duck's strong wing muscles as they beat, the lightness and goodness of flight. He reveled in the cool rush of wind through its feathers.

He adjusted the wings and let himself plummet down into the fogbank. Emerging over the village, he spotted the hut he shared with Squamiset and Natoncks. He'd never seen it from this angle, of course— it looked like a round wasp's nest made of matted reeds—but he recognized it by its location, standing a little apart from the other huts beside a high dune. He aimed for the square smoke hole, flapping his wings to brake and moderate his speed.

Inside the dwelling, he flapped in to perch with surprising accuracy upon one of Squamiset's hanging baskets. Sitting on the floor sorting a pile of freshly picked herbs were four very familiar people: Squamiset, Natoncks, Mishannock, and Shambisqua. The old man glanced up at the basket, showing no surprise. He gave Will a satisfied nod and turned his attention back to the work of sorting the herbs and tying them in bundles with blades of limber grass. Squamiset murmured something to the others, and all three turned their gazes up to Will, beaming fondly. Shambisqua's crooked-toothed smile was as radiant as ever. Remembering the humble form that he occupied at the moment, Will felt shy, but it didn't matter. These people were his friends, very nearly his adopted family. In their smiles he could see for the first time that they valued him not according to what he could or could not do— whether he could hunt or fish or perform magic or travel outside his body—but for his essential self, for the contents of his heart and spirit. It was a joyous, liberating realization.

After a time, he flapped the duck's wings and launched himself out through the smoke hole and away. The fog closed in around him, but it didn't matter. He knew his way back to the hidden dell. Soon he could see the little tea-colored pond beside which his own body lay unconscious on the mossy ground. He circled and flew in at a low angle, splashing down in the center of the pond and drifting to a stop.

The ripples in the pond subsided, and the duck slipped back into the reeds. Will opened his eyes, sat up, and stretched his arms above his head. All was as it should be. And he no longer doubted the existence of the Manitoo.

The next day, Will finally mastered one of Squamiset's lessons. That morning, with the old man looking on approvingly, he managed to move a strand of seaweed across a beach in a nonexistent breeze. Two days later, he caused a clamshell to croak the old man's name. His out-of-body experience with the duck seemed to have shaken something loose within him. On subsequent days, he amused Natoncks and Shambisqua by briefly creating the image of a dog dancing on its hind legs in a field of dried cornstalks. He caused the one-eyed *powwaw* Askooke, who had been so hostile to him upon his arrival but was now a friend, to shout in joy at the sight of a phantom moose galloping across a beach.

Will finally understood what Squamiset had been trying to tell him. There were no moose on the island, although there had been plenty near Askooke's childhood village on the mainland. Illusions made use of the relationship between the imagination and deeply instinctual emotions like fear and desire. People saw what they wanted to see— or what they dreaded seeing. Find out what moves a man, Squamiset said, and his own mind will do the work for you. The Sight was a different matter. Will didn't yet understand how that worked—and how it was possible that he could have left his body to take flight in the form of the duck. On the other hand, he no longer doubted the validity of Squamiset's visions, or his own.

Fourteen

On a morning in what Will believed was mid-October—he'd long since lost track of the English calendar—the people of Wannasquam held a ball game against the inhabitants of the island's other major village. The contest took place on a broad beach within the sheltered harbor on a field delineated by goals fashioned from upright whale jaws through which the ball had to be kicked or hit with the palm of one's hand. The day was calm, hazy, and mild for the time of year. Most of the young and middle-aged men from both villages took part. They wore nothing but breechcloths, and their faces and chests were painted with bold designs meant to frighten or intimidate the other team. A crowd of spectators lined the dunes overlooking the beach.

It was a far rougher game than Will had expected from such gentle people, and nothing at all like the games he and the other English boys had played in New Meadow. The players shoved and elbowed and let out ululating war cries as they fought for a chance to kick or slap the ball. Often they collided, knocking each other to the sand. In the shallow water at the edge of the harbor wrestling matches broke out, with dozens of splashing combatants. It was more like a bruising battle than a game, and it occurred to Will that this was exactly the point. The annual tradition was meant to replace and prevent actual bloodshed. Neither side had a clear advantage. The ball lurched down the beach indecisively, first one way, then the other. There were periods of stasis between charges and retreats, often filled with thunderous war songs and chanting. The teams relied on feints and strategies to advance the ball toward the other side's goal. The morning wore on until, around midday, in a single instant, everything changed.

Will, bruised and pleasantly exhausted, was jogging along on the firm sand beside Natoncks. Wannasquam had a slight advantage, and they were closer to the other village's goal than they had been all day. And then the moment came. The spectators let out a collective gasp, and Will looked up. His eyes followed the other players' shocked gazes out over the harbor. The ball meandered down to the waterline, forgotten. The harbor on this mild day was calm as glass, a great liquid mirror lapping up against the beach, with low dunes and the black fringe of a dwarf pine forest marking the opposite shore. Into the midst of this placid scene, its off-white canvas sails snapping in the breeze like a set of triangular clouds, sailed a Bermuda-rigged English schooner.

"God save us," Will said, forgetting himself. His limbs tingled with fear. The schooner shimmered like a vision from a long-ago daydream: raked masts, a jib attached to the jutting bowsprit, three slack sails blazing gold in the early autumn sun as the schooner's crew set about furling them. The canvas looked fresh, unstained by any long voyage, and in the end this might have been what kept Will from recognizing the ship's familiar outlines. The hull was newly painted navy blue with canary-yellow detailing. It was smartly built, shaped more like a knife than a tub to give it plenty of speed in a favorable wind. The vessel was outfitted for battle, with small brass cannons, three to a side, swivel guns mounted fore and aft, and a festive navy blue pennant streaming from the topmast. The colors of the King of England flew from the bowsprit, fluttering primly in the breeze.

As they recovered from their shock, the spectators began to flee, women and children hurrying back to the safety of the villages. Most of the players remained on the beach, drawing back from the tideline as if seawater had suddenly turned into an element they couldn't trust. Will stood with the men who had become his friends. It was strange to think that many of them were seeing an English ship for the first time. Some of the bolder players were already grabbing their bows and wading out into the harbor to threaten the intruders. Natoncks moved to join them, but Will grabbed his arm, shaking his head to remind him that he was a well-known renegade. But the truth was, the Misquinnipack looked so much like an islander by this time that an English sea captain would be hard-pressed to pick him out of the crowd. Will himself was another matter, of course. Squamiset caught his eye and gestured toward a hiding place behind a low dune where Will could observe without being spotted.

A fleet of half a dozen *mishoons*, with Squamiset in the prow of the first, struck out across the glassy harbor to intercept the schooner. Will supposed this made sense because he was the only one here who could serve as an effective translator, but it filled him with worry. An elderly Indian speaking fluent English and wearing a faded red horseman's jacket three or four decades out of fashion was likely to be noticed. Will's stomach churned. There was no doubt in his mind that he was the cause of this disruption and that the ship's crew had somehow found its way to this heretofore unknown island because Will had found his way before them. Squamiset glanced back, searching out Will's eyes across the water. He gave a small nod, and Will perceived the old man's voice ringing out within the stream of his own thoughts: *Courage, my friend.*

Approaching the schooner, the *mishoons* fanned out to keep their distance in a cautious formation. Lining the ship's high deck was the crew: a dozen weather-beaten European and African faces, most wearing woolen Monmouth caps. They bristled with armaments: pikes, long-barreled flintlocks with bayonets attached, and trumpet-barreled blunder-busses gaping like deadly, toothless mouths. Someone spoke a word in Algonkian. Ashore and on the *mishoons*, bows and arrows were raised. A polyphonic click of metal rang out across the water as the English firearms were cocked and aimed down over the gunwales. Back in the dunes, Will's heart knocked in his chest like a tolling bell. A brisk English voice called out. Will stared out across the water with a sudden feeling of vertigo.

The speaker hailed the men in the approaching *mishoons* again, repeating a demand whose meaning had not yet registered with Will, in part because the voice was so profoundly familiar. Will hadn't heard much English lately—for the most part Squamiset insisted on speaking to him in Algonkian—and it took him a moment to make sense of it. Reeling, he reached out for a hank of dune grass to steady himself. The voice was slightly distorted by the distance, but there was no mistaking it. It belonged to his older brother, Zeke.

"Will Poole? Is it truly you, Will?" Zeke Poole peered down from the schooner's deck, a note of hopeful incredulity in his voice as it carried over the calm harbor.

"Greetings, brother," Will said, panting from the effort of paddling his *mishoon* out to the schooner as fast as the resistance of the glassy water would allow. All eyes were upon him, from Zeke's motley crewmen with their muskets and woolen caps to the festively painted islanders sitting tensely in their *mishoons*, arrows nocked and pointed up at the Englishmen. "How did you find me?"

"But I hardly recognize you!" Zeke said, smiling. "You're all grown up." He wore a red Spanish-style flatcap and a mariner's long coat, navy blue with ivory piping and polished silver buttons. He looked well, ruddy and freckled from the sun, with a fashionably pointed blonde beard. His was a broad, honest face, one that called to mind so many of Will's childhood memories: Zeke rowing the skiff across the harbor to the oyster beds; Zeke teaching him to tie knots and hammer pegs; Zeke and his father stealing him away from schoolwork for a week's adventure up the Connecticut River in a homemade shallop. Then again, the circumstances of this reunion were not ideal. Will couldn't ignore the tense postures of his friends in the *mishoons* or the gaping barrels of the muskets and blunderbusses pointing downward from the schooner's deck. Zeke's arrival was seen as a grave crisis for the islanders. More *mishoons* were arriving every minute from the beach. More arrows were nocked and aimed. "Can you have some of these canoes dispersed, Will? My men are nervous, and I would ask them to put down their bows."

Will looked around helplessly. He imagined that the islanders must appear outlandish and barbaric to the Englishmen. Most, including Will, were naked but for loincloths. Some had chests dyed bloodred with a pigment derived from swamp maple bark. Some had styled their faces like skulls, bone white with soot rubbed into the eye sockets. Others had their scalps half shaven or sported bristling deer hair headdresses and toothed shark jaws tied into their topknots. Will himself had the tail feathers of a marsh hawk braided into his queue, and his face was divided by vertical black stripes. It was a wonder Zeke had even recognized him.

"If I may, young sir," Squamiset prompted. "Tell your crew to lower their pieces first."

Zeke raised his eyebrows, as surprised as Will had once been to hear a savage speak such flawless English. But he gave the order, and, after another tense moment, the muskets were lowered. Squamiset spoke to the men in his *mishoon*. One of them shouted out a short phrase in Algonkian. Bowstrings were relaxed, arrows were placed back into quivers, and within a few moments all but Squamiset's and Will's *mishoons* were headed for shore. "Are you the Wampanoag conjurer our governor is so up in arms about?" Zeke asked. "Never mind, of course you are. Greetings. You have my gratitude for keeping my brother alive and healthy." He returned his gaze to Will. "I suppose this old fellow is a more engaging tutor than James Overlock, though I don't imagine the two of you have been spending many hours poring over the Geneva Bible, hey?"

Will tried to match his brother's merry grin. The mention of Overlock and of Governor Rockingham had caused a sinking feeling in his stomach.

"Come aboard and let me show you the improvements to our old *Polly*," Zeke suggested, resting his arms on the gunwale. "She's a true fighting ship now, Will, quick as ever, and you still own a share in her. Let's catch up over a cup of claret."

Will tried to gauge Squamiset's brooding expression. The sight of an English ship in this sheltered harbor must have filled the old man with worries that would not easily be dispelled. "I think it would be better to meet ashore," he said.

"Very well." Zeke stood at the rail and barked out a series of orders, his tone shifting from that of a jocular youth to that of a ship's master accustomed to being obeyed. A tender was lowered over the side, and Zeke, along with three of his crewmen, dropped into it. One man—an enormous hulking Dutchman whom Will recognized as Jan van Loon, a man Zeke had taken several years before on a trading voyage to New Amsterdam—took the oars to row the tublike wherry ashore.

The village elders agreed that Zeke could accompany Will to his *wetu* if the rest of his crewmen remained aboard the schooner. The three loyal crewmen who'd come ashore to protect their master were not pleased by these conditions, but Zeke insisted, and the crewmen rowed the wherry back out to the *Polly*. Will and Zeke strolled behind the others, Zeke recounting his late voyage to the French Sugar Islands, the *Polly* loaded with pelts of beaver and sable and salt cod packed in spruce boughs. On the return, she'd carried cotton, salt, coffee, good French cloth, molasses, and rum. Zeke had profited enough on the sale of these goods in the markets of New Amsterdam and Massachusetts Bay to pay for the complete refurbishing of the *Polly*. "She's not only prettier," he remarked, "but well armed in case I run into a vindictive Frenchman or a Spaniard weighed down with gold."

Will laid out the true circumstances, as he saw them, of his imprisonment and escape from New Meadow, quite a different version, of course, than the one Zeke had heard from Overlock. It was a good thing Zeke wasn't a particularly devout Puritan. He was a merchant-adventurer, pure and simple, and he valued liberty and family bonds above piety and conformity. He had no trouble believing Will's story or sympathizing with the choices he'd made. Yet indeed, here on the island, with his scarlet flatcap and long blue mariner's coat, Zeke was a strange and frightening apparition. As they strode into the village, women gathered up their children and disappeared into their huts. Men and boys stood gripping bows and harpoons as the party passed, their faces hard. The dangerous reputation of English shipmasters was well known among the people of the island and, as Squamiset himself could attest, amply justified by history. Zeke's rolling gait and beaming gregariousness, Will knew, would only serve to increase the islanders' anxiety.

Squamiset appeared unperturbed by the tension gripping the village. Will tried to take a similarly heedless attitude, but it was difficult. He had the feeling—without any particular evidence for it—that everyone in the village must be angry with him. And he knew that if anything were to go wrong from this point forward, it truly *would* be his fault, whether or not the islanders chose to blame him. He distracted himself by attempting to see the village from Zeke's perspective. How primitive they all must look to him, these half-naked savages living in huts made of reeds and bent saplings—conditions any self-respecting Englishman would consider the most abject poverty. Will bristled at this thought. It was true that the islanders didn't build grand houses or horde their possessions, but in other ways they were more than rich. Wannasquam was self-sufficient. There was plenty of food and ample time for leisure, depending on the season. Will had yet to see anyone living in misery, something that could not be said of most English settlements.

A group of children, their curiosity overcoming their fear, came over to fondle the rich fabric of Zeke's Spanish breeches. Zeke paused, bending to show them the shining silver buttons on his coat.

Will stopped at the *wetu* he shared with Squamiset and Natoncks and indicated the hut with a wave of his hand. "Home sweet home." He watched his brother's carefully neutral face as he ran his eyes over the rounded hivelike structure sheathed in mats of woven reeds. There was a new scar at the corner of his left eye that Will hadn't noticed before, small and white and shaped like a fingernail or a scimitar. At that moment Shambisqua walked up to deliver a bundle of freshly harvested herbs to Squamiset. Zeke, ever the gentleman, swept off the flatcap with a flourish, dropped to one knee, and held out his hand. Shambisqua, alarmed, hugged the herbs to her chest. "She doesn't understand what you want," Will explained. "It is not their custom to take hands."

Zeke got to his feet and bowed his head respectfully. "Greetings, dear lady."

Shambisqua stared at him, then, helplessly, looked to Will. He tried to make his expression reassuring. Zeke was a good man with the best of intentions. Squamiset took the herbs from Shambisqua, and they set off together toward her grandmother's hut. When they were gone, Will ushered Zeke inside. "The girl is delightful," Zeke said, taking a seat on the sleeping platform. "Won't she join us?"

"She speaks little English. And you, even less Algonkian."

"Well, it brightens my day to see her. She is yours?"

Will felt his ears redden. "No, not mine. She's an apprentice to her grandmother, a very skilled healer."

"Studying to be a medicine woman, is she? Fascinating. Well, I'd say you're developing fine taste in women." He glanced around the *wetu*, taking in the drying herb bundles, the pelt-strewn sleeping platforms, the firepit with its mound of white cinders partially illuminated by the parallelogram of sunlight slanting in through the smoke hole. "And you seem healthy enough," he added, turning his appraising gaze back to his younger brother. "It's good to see that the savages have been feeding you."

Will frowned. *Savages.* It was a word he had used often enough himself, and he wouldn't have thought twice about it just a few months ago. Still, it didn't feel like the right word to describe his friends now: Squamiset, Natoncks, Shambisqua, or any of the people of Wannasquam.

"The *powwaw* seems an interesting fellow. Squamiset, is it?"

Will nodded. "He's considered a great man among these people, Zeke, a wise counselor and a visionary. We've become the best of friends, you know. If it weren't for him, I'd be dead."

"I don't doubt it."

They passed a moment in silence. From the pocket of his jacket, Zeke removed a small clay pipe of the sort that was the fashion among seafaring men. He packed the bowl with tobacco and used his knife to pluck an ember from the fire to light it. Will asked, "How did you manage to find me?"

"Oh, it was easy enough," Zeke replied, puffing on the pipe. "Word of a young Englishman dwelling on an unmapped island came to Mayhew, at Martha's Vineyard. He passed it on to Reverend Williams at Narragansett Bay, and I got word of it one day at the Fort Saybrook trading post. I sailed over to Martha's Vineyard and tracked down Deacon Mayhew himself, who conjectured that you were on this island, which he'd never visited but suspected to be fifteen or twenty miles east of him. Apparently there are praying Indians in his flock who paddle out to the southwestern tip of this island once or twice a year to trade. So you see, Will, you weren't as well hidden as you thought."

Will absorbed this news. If Zeke could find him with so little trouble, it seemed inevitable that other English ships would follow. And when they did, the spell of splendid isolation that had protected the island would be broken. Disaster would ensue, and it would be Will's fault.

Zeke gave his younger brother a sympathetic look. "It wasn't a bad idea to come here, but you couldn't expect to remain safe forever. An English renegade living among savages is like a festering splinter to a zealot like John Rockingham. The kind of infection that can only be cleared up by drawing the splinter out and tossing it into the fire. Do you see what I mean? You're lucky I found you first."

Will's cheeks burned. "Why should Rockingham care? Why can't he just leave me alone and tend to his worldly ambitions? Lord knows he has plenty of them."

Zeke, exasperated, gazed at him. "*Think* for a moment, Will. He can't allow a New Meadow man to live happily among savages. What if others were to follow your example?"

"The world would be a better place, in my opinion."

"Don't be thickheaded. Rockingham and his allies don't see it that way, and they never will."

Zeke got up and squatted to knock the ashes from his pipe at the edge of the firepit. He came back to sit on the platform next to Will and leaned forward, clapping a hand on Will's knee. "New Amsterdam is governed by the Dutch, Will. Rockingham has no jurisdiction. You'll need a new name and a new identity. It's becoming quite the prosperous little city. You'll be my factor there. Help me bring goods to market."

"No." Will shook his head vehemently. "I can't do that."

"Well then, if you prefer, there's the Barbadoes. Plenty of opportunities there, and beautiful women. I could even be convinced to return you to Old England, Will, if that idea appeals to you more, although there is a civil war on and you'd have to be careful. You could try to lay claim to our father's estates in Devonshire, God rest his soul. But whatever you do, you must leave this place immediately, before Rockingham finds you."

Will gazed into the dying fire, his shoulders drooping. Zeke was only trying to look out for him, as any good brother would. For an instant his mind conjured up his own severed head, pale and sickly green, like the illusion Squamiset had made for the bird hunter, plunking on the close-cropped grass of the New Meadow common and rolling to a stop at the booted feet of Governor Rockingham. He shook his head to rid himself of the gruesome image. Zeke sighed in frustration. "Be sensible, Will. Good God, you're living a dream here. It cannot last. You must come away with me now. We'll take your tawny beauty with us, if that's what's holding you up."

"It's not that," Will said. "Leaving this island now would be akin to cutting out my heart. These are my people now, Zeke. If not in blood, then in spirit."

Zeke eyed him, puffing on the pipe. "You're not only dressing up like a savage, brother. You're starting to *talk* like one."

Will smiled ruefully. "I need to think it over, Zeke. Let me walk you back to the harbor."

It was dusk when they stood on the beach. Zeke waved to his crewmen, and the two brothers stood gazing out on the anchored *Polly*. She was a pretty sight, Will had to admit, floating high upon the glassy harbor with all three sails neatly furled, the length of her elegant hull burnished red and gold in the failing sun. The wherry slid in, rasping on the sand. Will greeted Jan van Loon and the other crewmen and bid his elder brother good-night. Zeke adjusted his flatcap and stepped into the boat. He didn't look back as the broad-shouldered Dutchman rowed him out to the *Polly*.

Will did not sleep well, tossing and turning on his reed mat under his furs. The idea of leaving filled him with gloom. Despite Squamiset's consistent warnings against it, he'd become attached to this sea-washed island where the fog rolled in and the breakers roared and the sun bathed the hills in milky golden light. He had interests here, not least among them a beautiful oval-faced girl with sad intelligent eyes and slightly crooked teeth. He understood Zeke's point that remaining in place was dangerous, but he couldn't imagine actually sailing out of the harbor and never coming back. Hearing Natoncks's light snores but sensing that Squamiset was awake, he whispered to the old man across the hut. "There's something I don't understand about your visions."

"Yes?" came the soft-voiced answer.

"You claim they have directed us to the home of Cautántowwit, in the southwest. So why did we come to *this* island, so far to the east? Why did we not strike out over land, for example, into the wild interior? Would that not have been the straightest way to the southwest?"

"To attempt such a direct route to Sowwaniu would have invited a premature end to our journey. Beyond the river of the Iroquois are the Mauquawogs, the Mitukmechakik, and the Tree-Eaters, all enemies of our coastal people. They are numerous in the mountains, and some of them would like to take out our hearts and feast upon them. You are right, Will, that we shall eventually have to go west as well as south. But we had to come here first. It has provided us a safe haven, and we have found a good home for Natoncks."

"Yes. And I thought *we'd* found a good home too." Will couldn't keep the bitterness from his voice. The old man was silent. "Once we've gone to see Cautántowwit," Will asked after a moment, "will it be possible for us to return here?"

"It is improbable," the old man replied gently.

"Then it astounds me how casually you throw away your happiness!"

Squamiset hesitated, his face hidden in darkness. "Of what importance is happiness to an old man, Will? I will be happy when my destiny is complete. I will be happy when I have brought you to Sowwaniu."

Will stared up at a patch of bright stars visible through the smoke hole. He didn't understand how he had arrived at this pass, where he was apparently required to put aside the best things he'd ever encountered in life. He had the sensation of being carried downstream on a fast current, away from everything he'd come to love, toward an abyss of emptiness, loneliness, and danger. And there didn't seem to be anything he could do about it.

Fifteen

In the morning Will sat cross-legged on the spongy moss in the hidden dell. The duck dabbled around the edge of the pond. It stopped periodically to plunge its snow-white head beneath the water, tail straight up, as it foraged for shoots and pondweed.

After a time Will lay back, closed his eyes, and tried to clear his mind of thoughts. It was no good. He sat up and spoke to the duck. "Will you not grant me the Sight? I wish to see the future." There was no glimmer of understanding from the duck, which seemed utterly absorbed in its dabbling. Will lay back again to stare up at the sky. Clouds streamed overhead, their shapes shifting and re-forming as they moved: a turtle, a whale, a maple leaf, a dragon. Watching them brought to mind his old dream of flying. In the dream it had always been a matter of trust, he remembered, and a certain dash of blind optimism. If the wind was right, you just leapt up into it and there you were. He began to feel drowsy. His eyelids closed, and suddenly he found himself floating on the glassy surface of the pond. He beat his wings, sprinting across the water, and caught a wind gust. The pond and the treetops of the hidden dell receded beneath him, and then he was flying above the rolling moors.

He flew north across the island, over the village with its reed-mat beehive dwellings emitting slanted ribbons of smoke, over the hills and bluffs that sheltered the harbor where the *Polly* lay at anchor. But there was something different about the *Polly*. And then he saw that it wasn't

Zeke's festively painted schooner at all but a much larger vessel, a massive frigate with dozens of square-mounted sails furled on three tall masts newly blackened with tar. The hull was painted glossy black with a stripe of crimson just above the waterline. A long pennant streamed from the mainmast, and the King's colors flew from a jackstaff mounted to the bowsprit. The ship had a figurehead above its cutwater, a larger-than-life angel with a long silent trumpet. Orderly piles of trade goods glinted on the quarterdeck: iron blades and cookpots, bolts of cloth, mirrors, beads, and small casks or firkins of rum. He made a wide circle around the frigate, flapping his duck wings and steering with his tail. Beyond the afterdeck, inside the window to the master's cabin, he spotted two blurred figures bent over a table.

He heard a powder charge, and a whistling ball displaced the air beside his head. He was so surprised that he nearly plummeted into the sea; a soldier on the quarterdeck had fired the musket, no doubt envisioning roast duck for supper. Will beat his wings, circling higher. The light changed, and suddenly the frigate burst into flames. It was only then that the truth of what he was seeing sank in. The Manitoo's wings had borne him forward through time as well as space. The scene had changed because the future was subject to change. He was witnessing the highly conditional world of events that had not yet come to pass.

The harbor was empty now, calm and pristine, with no English ship in sight, not even the *Polly*. Will flew over the island to an empty beach on the south shore, where the breakers drew and redrew a fringe of lacy sea foam. Soothed by this familiar sight, he wheeled north again to get a look at the village. But to his horror, the village had changed. There was rubbish strewn about, shells and bones and discarded cloth. A few of the huts had fallen into disrepair, and in the center of the village an enormous pile of dying cinders let off a greasy, foul-smelling ribbon of smoke. A group of young men caroused in a weed-choked cornfield, looking slow and peevish. They wore Monmouth caps pulled down over their foreheads like loutish sailors. One held a cutlass; he waved it up at Will with an unsteady, menacing swagger. Among this sullen mob were half a dozen boys whom Will had become friendly with over months of fishing and foraging. Other than the drunken cutlass-wielder, none raised their eyes.

The light changed again. Early autumn faded to late autumn, a cold day in November or perhaps December. A sharp northwest wind blew in off the ocean, and the surface of the freshwater pond had taken on the opacity of hammered steel. In the village most of the huts were in disrepair, and some had collapsed in on themselves. There was no evidence of activity: no one making nets or weirs, no cookfires, no children playing in the barren gardens. A northwest wind howled across an island that seemed devoid of life.

Will was so heartbroken he could barely stay aloft. He flapped back toward the hidden forest where his sleeping body awaited him. Was this the future? Was he the cause of it?

That evening Will and Squamiset walked down to the harbor. Zeke rowed himself ashore, and the three held council among the dunes. They agreed to sail on the next outgoing tide, just after dawn on the following morning. They all shook hands, and Zeke rowed himself back out to the *Polly*. Squamiset headed back to the village to inform Wequashim. Will took a much longer route home, over the moors to the hidden dell, because he was in a state of emotional shock and needed time alone to think. At the pond he sat cross-legged on the moss and stared into the black bottomless depths. It did not give him peace. He was sure that he and Squamiset were making the right choice for the people of the island, but it was a choice that filled him with despair.

They had few possessions, so there was little packing to be done. The most difficult task was the simple act of saying good-bye. Squamiset went to sit with Wequashim and his three elderly wives, and Will went to the healer's hut. Shambisqua was out gathering on the moors. Mishannock put her hand to his cheek and invited him inside for a bowl of steaming clam broth. Will's Algonkian wasn't good enough to explain precisely why he and Squamiset were leaving, but the old woman clearly understood.

His resolve not to succumb to his emotions broke at dawn the next day as he and Natoncks and Squamiset strode across the broad beach at the edge of the harbor. It was the same beach where the festive ball game had taken place only a few days earlier, but for Will the intervening days had painted it in a sorrowful light, as if each gentle wavelet breaking on the shell-strewn sand was a symbol of lost love and broken bonds. And what on any other day might have been a glorious sight—the brightly painted *Polly* riding in the glassy harbor, its crisp white canvas in the process of being unfurled and shaken out for sailing—made him feel nothing but desperation and heartsickness.

Zeke was sensitive enough not to send the wherry. Half a dozen *mishoons* lay with their hulls up on the beach, among them Squamiset's old dugout with the carving of the osprey on its weathered prow. It had washed ashore on a remote beach on the eastern end of the island, and the one-eyed *powwaw* Askooke, in a gesture of solidarity and friendship, had secretly retrieved it for them. He'd dried it out by his fire, added some of his own mysterious snakelike carvings for luck, oiled it, and presented it to Squamiset and Will the previous evening as a parting gift.

Shambisqua stood beside her grandmother on the beach. As Will approached, she pressed her hand to her heart, and he embraced her. Their lips touched for a moment—hers warm and soft as satin—and then she stepped back, averting her gaze. Tears welled up, blurring Will's vision. He turned to Mishannock. The old woman's eyes brimmed with pride and affection for him, strengthening his conviction that he was choosing the right course. To one-eyed Askooke and Squamiset's old cousin, Wequashim, he merely nodded. Both men put their hands to their hearts to show their respect for the sacrifice he was making. When it came time to take leave of Natoncks, Will's throat tightened further, though he was determined not to shed tears. "Be well, my friend," he said in Algonkian.

"Careful, Toyusk," Natoncks replied in English. "Protect, help old man." Will nodded. It was the longest English speech that Will had ever heard from him; though it was a little scrambled, he understood it well enough.

Squamiset surprised Will by stepping up to the *mishoon*'s prow instead of taking his usual place in the stern. It was gesture of confidence, and Will felt duly honored. Glancing back at Shambisqua one more time, he pushed the *mishoon* out from the shallows, hoisting himself aboard as the dugout knifed out into deeper water. He picked up a paddle and steered a course to meet the *Polly*, which was already slipping with the tide out toward the mouth of the harbor.

Sixteen

The *Polly's* sails snapped and her masts creaked as she emerged from the harbor mouth into the sound and tacked west along the island's low shoreline. When the schooner had cleared the sandbars off the southwestern point, the deck began to roll with the swells of the open ocean. Zeke joined Will at the stern rail, handing him a pewter cup filled with claret wine. "A brisk sail, God willing, shall lighten your mood."

Will nodded, glancing away so that his brother wouldn't see the mist of tears blurring his eyes. He kept himself steady by clutching a sheet line as he gazed back at the island, a diminishing strip of sand crested by the low green haze of the moorlands, and tried not to think about the fact that he would almost certainly never set foot upon those shores again. He took a small measure of solace in the knowledge that Natoncks, after coming so close to losing his head, had a new chance at life now. As for Shambisqua, she would likely be better off without him. But leaving her had created an ache in his chest that felt permanent, like a gun worm driven into his heart.

Zeke went off to attend to the ship, and Squamiset came to take his place. Naturally, he didn't need to cling to the sheets or the rail to steady himself, as Will did. It was altogether remarkable, Will mused, that a man could be so ancient and yet so lithe and solid on his feet. Together they gazed back at the receding island. It was now just a low smudge on the horizon, like a fading dream. "Good things do not last forever, Will."

"I know."

"You are young," Squamiset said. "You cannot see as far as an old crow like me. But you have learned much, and Natoncks is safe. We lived well on the island. It was not wasted time."

"I know."

A steady northwest wind plucked foam from the crests of the sea-green swells that glittered merrily in the midmorning sun. After a period of mild queasiness Will was already becoming accustomed to the creaking undulation of the schooner. After a few days aboard, like an old salt, he supposed he would find the constant motion reassuring. The *Polly* was a pleasant and finely crafted ship: open to the air, driven by the wind, enclosed by nothing but snapping sailcloth and taut riggings of pine-blacked hemp. The deck was broad and dry, bathed in fresh sea air and warmed by pleasant early autumn sunshine. It was perfect weather for sailing, Will told himself, but as much as he tried, he couldn't give himself over to the simple joys of living. The ocean around the schooner was barren and endless, a vast green flood drowning the populated earth, just as Will felt, out of moral necessity, that he had just finished drowning his best chance at happiness.

A brief time later, a ship appeared on the horizon. It was too distant to see in detail, but there was something troubling about the fact that they were seeing it now, just as they were losing sight of the island. The ship was on a northeasterly course heading toward precisely where the *Polly* had come from: the island itself. A chill ran up and down Will's spine.

Confirming his worst fears, the *Polly*'s helmsman soon identified the ship as a twenty-gun frigate that had been delivered across the Atlantic two weeks earlier from a shipyard in Portsmouth, England, and now belonged to Governor John E. Rockingham of New Meadow. Will stood at the schooner's starboard gunwale peering through Zeke's spyglass. The frigate was dark and tall with three high masts. He imagined that it must have dwarfed the other vessels moored in the harbor at New

Meadow, like a great black swan towering over a gaggle of dun-colored ducklings. It had a high poop deck and a pronounced beakhead, giving it the shape of an angular, upturned crescent. True to his duck-borne vision, the hull was black with a stripe of crimson above the waterline, and a long scarlet pennant flew from the mainmast. Through the glass, Will could make out a crowd of helmets beetling in the shadows beneath the sails and a long row of cannon muzzles peering out through the shadowy gun ports in the lower deck. The frigate's many sails luffed in the wind as it began, unmistakably, to alter its bearing. It had spotted the *Polly* and was coming to intercept them.

When Zeke gave the order to put on more sail, his crewmen looked at him with trepidation. This was a twenty-gun frigate, after all, manned by a crew of experienced sailors and carrying a large contingent of New Meadow militiamen. The *Polly* didn't stand a chance if she were to be caught, and everyone knew it. But these were loyal men, and they knew Zeke well enough to understand that he would never willingly surrender his own brother. After a moment's hesitation, they sprang to their tasks.

Jan van Loon was Zeke's first mate and helmsman. The rest of the crew were a few African freedmen and half a dozen English drifters culled from the wharves and customhouses of Boston and New Amsterdam. When prodded into action they were an efficient lot; in a few short moments the *Polly* had all her sails taut to the wind, her hull slicing through the glittering swells as fast as she could go.

She was much smaller and lighter than the frigate, and the ability to get a quick lead was one of her few advantages. Zeke had set them a south-westerly course, away from the island. The Governor's black frigate followed tightly enough, however, and Will kept borrowing Zeke's spyglass to gaze back at it. It was an impressive ship, the wind spreading its square sails, the royal flag of union and the scarlet pennant of Rockingham's private trading company streaming from the mainmast. Above where the cutwater sliced the translucent swells perched the larger-than-life figurehead that Will remembered from his vision: the avenging angel leaning forward into the wind as it blew its silent trumpet.

His heart skipped a beat as he recognized Governor Rockingham's distinctive silver beard among the glinting helmets and corselets on the poop deck. Rockingham walked with a peculiar gait, quick and smooth-soled, as if he were rolling on wheels across the deck. He came to stand at the taffarel, the highest point on the frigate's towering poop deck, and adjusted the black-plumed cavalier's hat that had once rested like a shadow on the floorboards of Will's childhood home. The Governor's distinguished face was ruddy in the cool wind, his cape flapping behind him as he stood. A soldier handed him a spyglass, and he scanned the *Polly*'s deck. The round lens winked and jerked to a stop when it came to Will, and in that instant they were staring at each other across the swells. Reeling from the shock of this sudden encounter, Will lowered Zeke's spyglass. When he lifted it back up, the Governor was no longer there.

Squamiset had come aft to stand beside Will at the bulwark. He stared out over the water at the chasing ship. "You know this may not go well, don't you? That beyond a certain point, not even the most successful of my illusions can save us?"

Will nodded. Suddenly, compared to the sleek and well-armed power of the Governor's frigate, Squamiset's powers seemed limited, even whimsical.

The *Polly* was a sleek ship, however, and Zeke was a gifted mariner with numerous tricks to play. They tacked and came about, taking advantage of the shifting wind to force the frigate into cumbersome maneuvers. Several times that afternoon and evening, they actually lost sight of it over the horizon. But each time it reappeared, black-hulled and pinch-bodied like a colossal wasp as it chased the *Polly* over the wind-ruffled swells.

The pursuit continued throughout that night and into the next day. In the middle of the afternoon the wind turned north and west. This was calamitous for the *Polly* on her current bearing, and the frigate began to gain steadily. The dread aboard the schooner was as palpable as a smell. "We'll lead them ashore and do our best to lose them," Zeke announced. "If we find a river deep enough to sail up they'll try to trap us. Then perhaps we can slip by them in the night."

Soon they were close enough to land to pick out beaches and individual trees. The frigate was nearly upon them, but Zeke's luck was good; his lookout sighted a river delta just as darkness fell. The *Polly* changed course to sail up into it, and, rounding an oxbow, managed to escape the frigate's view. The river was deep enough for the *Polly* but shallow enough to force the frigate to anchor until morning, when Rockingham could send a tender upstream to sound the bottom. It was a long and tense night, but, just as Zeke had hoped, the *Polly* was able to whisper by under the cover of darkness and escape once again out to sea. Will clapped his brother on the back and shook Jan van Loon's gigantic hand. It looked as if they'd done it.

At dawn, however, the hopeful mood aboard the schooner was shattered. Like the black embodiment of an unshakeable nightmare, the tall-masted frigate loomed in the haze on the aft horizon. It seemed bigger than Will remembered, too, even from the day before. Aboard the *Polly*, all conversation ceased except for clipped orders from Zeke and the occasional grim observation from the old salts about the frigate's impressive armaments. Some of the younger crewmen were visibly nervous. Others glanced at Will with hooded eyes. If it weren't for him, they wouldn't have needed to risk their lives.

Just after noon, having re-closed the gap, the frigate began firing a chaser gun mounted to its forecastle. Zeke shouted out a series of orders and the *Polly* took evasive action, tacking nimbly this way and that, but the explosions shook the air, and the cannonballs from the chaser splashed to port and starboard. It was just a matter of time.

The first hit was a loud splintering crash into the *Polly's* mizzen-mast. The mast held, but a shard of pine careened out to hit van Loon, shucking deep into the flesh of his massive shoulder like an expertly thrown blade. Face drained of color but otherwise expressionless, the huge Dutchman pulled out the bloody splinter and tossed it over the gunwale into the sea. Zeke let out a string of curses, striding aft to look at the damaged mizzenmast. He came back shaking his head. "That's it. There's no way we can outrun them now."

"Strike your sails!" A thin shout came carrying across the swells. "Or we will not hesitate to send you to the bottom!"

Zeke issued another long string of profanity, but he didn't give the order to strike sails. The *Polly* cut through the swells, every inch of canvas flung to the wind despite the crippled mizzenmast. Perhaps they could find another harbor or river mouth too shallow for the frigate to enter, though as far as Will's eyes could see there was nothing but featureless coast: narrow beaches and low forest stretching in a flat line to both the north and the south.

The frigate's chasers kicked up another great fountain of water just feet from the *Polly's* bowsprit. As the gunners found their range, Will suspected that the shots would begin to hit their mark. Squamiset stood beside him at the aft bulwark, his head bowed and his eyes closed in deep concentration. Will felt a momentary surge of hope as the schooner's hull and weather deck began to take on a hint of the dancing translucent green of the surrounding ocean. But it was too little, too late. The frigate's next shot was a strike, punching a ragged hole just below the deck.

Another strike, this time a bar shot, splintered the base of *Polly's* mainmast, sending the mainsail crashing down in a great whistling rush of shrouds and sailcloth.

A stunned silence came over the crew. The game was up. They went through the motions of preparing for combat, but their efforts were half-hearted, slow and heavy in the shadow of what they were convinced was imminent death. The frigate was alongside the *Polly* now, its decks bristling with pikes and muskets, its big square sails flapping thunderously as the crew worked to the bosun's crisp orders. Will gazed at the mouths of carriage-mounted cannons looming out of the gun ports. A single order was all it would take. The *Polly* would be splintered into a million pieces. He braced himself, and he could sense Zeke and Squamiset and Jan van Loon doing the same.

A familiar patrician voice hailed them across the water. "Lay down your arms, and I shall be merciful!" Governor Rockingham stood at the taffarel. He looked somber and very tall in his black cloak and plumed hat, but his voice sounded reasonable, as if he wanted nothing more than a reasoned discussion on this sunny afternoon.

Aboard the *Polly*, all eyes swiveled to Zeke. For a moment his features flashed defiance, but this quickly faded. He knew his position was untenable. And he was already in mourning for his beautiful, damaged ship.

Will cleared his throat. He had the power to end this.

Seventeen

The frigate reeked of gunpowder and pine tar. Its decks bustled with activity as the Governor's bosun shouted orders, hordes of crewmen hauled in sheets and secured them, and hundreds of square yards of sailcloth tensed to the wind. Soldiers hustled the two prisoners up the gangway to the forecastle, where they were separated amidst a crowd of grinning sailors and militiamen. A raucous cheer went up as Squamiset was shoved forward to his knees at the bowsprit. Will, tense with foreboding, strained without success to see more as the militiamen hustled him aft toward the Governor's cabin.

Meanwhile, the *Polly*, dismasted and rudderless, floated slowly away from the frigate. It had been cast adrift on Rockingham's orders, and the Governor was no doubt glad to be rid of it. Towing a crippled ship all the way back to New Meadow would have been extremely time-consuming, and Rockingham's main concern at this point was Will, not his older brother. Besides, without sails to propel her, freedom was a cruel enough punishment for the *Polly* and her crew. The prevailing currents were already sweeping her north and east, farther out to sea. If she drifted too far, her rations would begin to dwindle. Things might get desperate for a time, though Will was confident it would end well. Zeke's crewmen were already lowering tenders and stringing hawsers for towlines. It would mean a lot of work, but eventually the tenders would be able to tow the *Polly* to shore. There they would set up a long-term camp, and Zeke's carpenter would direct the crew in felling logs and hewing planks to replace the masts and make other necessary repairs. Zeke would get the *Polly* back into working order, though it might take a month or more—so Will hoped. He wouldn't be around to see it and neither, unfortunately, would Squamiset, whom the Governor had taken prisoner along with Will.

Rockingham awaited him in the master's cabin, a pleasant low-ceilinged room illuminated by a row of divided-light windows with a view of the frigate's trailing wake. The Governor sat at a long table in the center of the room. His face was flushed from the sun and sea air, and his pale blue eyes flashed with triumph. He appeared to have lost a bit of hair since they'd last met; his fashionably long silver locks sprouted from a pallid dome that looked soft and vulnerable, like a hermit crab out of its shell. He'd placed the black-plumed cavalier's hat on the floor, exactly as he'd done in the parlor of Will's house. The sight of its velvety blackness deepened Will's dread.

He was so focused on the Governor that it took him a moment to notice the portly man sitting in the chair to Rockingham's left who was none other than James Overlock. Will was surprised to see him; the former steward must have wormed his way further into the Governor's good graces to secure an invitation on the new frigate's inaugural voyage. Overlock gazed up at him with an ambivalent half-smile, his small eyes gleaming. He looked prosperous in an embroidered doublet and falling lace collar, and he seemed to have gained weight: his face was jowlier than Will remembered, and, to comic effect in Will's opinion, he'd waxed his mustache and let his beard grow out to a point, very much like John Rockingham's. The Governor watched their eyes meet with a mix of curiosity and pleasure, as if arranging this little reunion had been the main purpose of his voyage.

"Am I to be allowed counsel?" Will asked. His words seemed to sink into the floorboards unanswered. Beyond the walls of the master's cabin, he could hear the bosun shouting and the cries of seagulls. From the direction of the forecastle there came a faint, ominous bout of laughter. The frigate creaked as its sailcloth responded to a slight shift in the wind. After a moment, Rockingham cleared his throat.

"I require you to abjure the savage religion, Will. Absolutely and with sincere conviction. If you do that, you shall be granted a period of meditation and prayer. And if, in that allotted time, you return to the Truth, with humility and sincerity, your life may be spared. Is that not good news?"

Will shook his head. "I wish to confirm that no harm will come to my friend before I discuss any of this. Bring him here, and the two of us will seek the good Lord's mercy together. This way you can save *two* souls, not just one."

Rockingham smiled sadly. "*Do* think carefully about it, Will, before this brief opportunity passes. I'm afraid you've already sacrificed your standing as a gentleman, along with any last claim to the family fortune. But you could still live as a craftsman or a laborer. Or perhaps as a school-teacher, given what Mr. Overlock tells me about your aptitude for letters."

Will glanced at Overlock, whose expression was carefully neutral. What was left of the Poole estate would certainly fall to him now, a reward for his slavish loyalty and a punishment for Zeke, who had risked so much on his brother's behalf. The ship's timbers creaked again, and the deck tipped up slightly into the wind. It wouldn't be long, a few days perhaps, before the frigate sailed beyond the scattering of barrier islands that protected the harbor of New Meadow. Will looked up. "I will accept your offer, Your Excellency, if you agree to give the old Wampanoag a similar chance."

Rockingham regarded him coldly. "The savage is a minion of Satan. As we speak in here, Captain Hooker is out on the deck attempting to learn what he knows that can be of use to us. When that is done, he has orders to dispose of him."

"Dispose of him?" Prickling needles of panic shot up and down Will's arms, accompanied by an undertow of red fury. "Then you'll have to dispose of me, too."

"Be careful what you wish for, Will. And I advise you to stop trying to intervene on the savage sorcerer's behalf; it does not help advance your case. Maybe God will forgive him. I cannot."

Will felt himself reddening; he leaned forward and strained against the manila cords that bound his wrists. "I spit in the eye of the bloodthirsty villain you call God."

Rockingham shook his head disbelievingly. Overlock, wide-eyed, blew out his cheeks. "What a horrid thing to say," Will's former guardian murmured.

"Bring him to the forecastle," Rockingham growled to the guards, his pale blue eyes merciless and flinty. "Let him witness Hooker's sport for a time. Then take him below and clap him in irons. Keep him secure at every moment, and don't give him the chance to struggle or attempt escape. I want him undamaged when we arrive in New Meadow."

A steady wind blew in from the southwest, frothing up whitecaps and hurrying little rafts of sea foam across the swells. On the way up to the forecastle the guards stopped to force a strip of sailcloth between Will's jaws, tying it tightly behind his neck so that he could no longer open or close his mouth. Squamiset was similarly gagged and bound at the wrists and ankles. Hooker had him laid out on the cathead, a stout timber projecting from the forecastle above the bowsprit. They'd stripped him of the old horseman's jacket; without it he looked frail and vulnerable, his fine silver hair half unbraided and fluttering in the wind and his back raw from whipping. Will struggled against the manila cords until the raw skin of his wrists started to bleed, but his efforts only provoked the guards to tighten their grip on him. Held immobile, he had no choice but to stare in horror at the abuse unfolding on the crowded forecastle.

Hooker stood over Squamiset with his cutlass raised, his boat-brimmed helmet resting on the planks beside him. His scarred cheeks were beaded with sweat, which had begun to pool and trickle down into his grey-flecked copper beard. The militia captain was whipping Will's old friend with the flat blade of the cutlass. Every time he brought the weapon down there was a shotlike slap, and Hooker grunted a little humorous phrase or aphorism that caused the men to laugh. Some laughed with abandon. Others laughed uneasily, as if they weren't quite sure that the flogging of an elderly man—even a savage warlock known to be in league with the Devil—was actually a matter for hilarity.

Will couldn't stand to watch. He closed his eyes, wracking his brain for some trick or illusion that would allow him to help Squamiset free himself. He could think of nothing, and when he opened his eyes he couldn't see if his old friend was still breathing. Tears streamed down his face. He mouthed a silent prayer to the Manitoo, and a moment later he detected movement around Squamiset's rib cage. The old man was still alive.

Hooker addressed the assembled men. "The warlock refuses to share his secrets. I think it's time we end his misery and send him down to his master's flaming lair!" A cheer went up. Some of the men cheered with abandon while others cheered halfheartedly, as if worried that they would be noticed if they did not. Governor Rockingham, meanwhile, had come to stand beside Will on the forecastle. He rested his hand companionably on Will's shoulder, as if he were a favorite uncle and the two of them were spectators at a country fair. Hooker glanced up to confirm his decision—the look in his pale grey eyes sent a shiver down Will's spine—and Rockingham, smiling benevolently, nodded his assent. Will tried to plead with Rockingham to end this brutality, but his words came through the gag as a plaintive, muffled gargle. The guards held him firmly in place. Squamiset was on the point of being killed, and there was absolutely nothing he could do.

He'd noticed a slight change in Squamiset's position. The old man had rolled over on his side and lifted his head as if to get a better view of the rest of the ship. In the next moment one of the sailors cried out in alarm, "Fire in the galley!"

Black smoke poured through a hatch in the foredeck. Several men rushed to raise the hatch, and half a dozen clambered down the ladder. The bosun shouted orders, forming the crew into a chain to hoist seawater in buckets and pass them down the hatch. But flames had now broken out on the opposite end of the ship, beyond the mizzenmast, licking out of the bulkhead of the Governor's cabin. Additional fires were spotted and shouted out: in the ship's lantern and the braces, in the orlop deck and the chicken coop.

Beside Will on the forecastle, Rockingham was red-faced, screaming orders at Hooker and the panicked bosun. Hooker, too, was distracted, his cutlass lowered and his big square head jerking this way and that as he yelled instructions to the men attempting to put out the fires. Those not bringing up seawater rushed around the decks, beating at the flames with jackets and hats, while seawater from canvas buckets splashed ineffectually upon one of the numerous small fires that had spring up all over the frigate. Will tried to take advantage of the chaos to escape from the guards, but they kept a tight hold on him, and he remained helpless, a passive observer. The fires had proliferated across the ship, and the flames had grown taller, livid and roaring. As soon as one was quenched another would flare up. It was as if a fungus of live embers had infected the body of the frigate, and the bright orange flames with their dark black smoke were its mushrooms. A few frightened sailors dove into the sea to avoid the horror of a floating inferno.

The Governor, finally having understood what was happening, ran around the deck cajoling the men to ignore the fires, even thrusting his bare hands into the flames to prove that the fires were illusory. Will could see the men slowly waking up as word spread across the frigate that the fires were producing no actual heat and doing no actual damage. Sailors began throwing lines to those in the water and hoisting them up to safety. Meanwhile, Rockingham had strode back up to the forecastle with his sword unsheathed, clearly intending to kill Squamiset where he lay. Will tried to shout out a warning, producing only a strangled gurgle. But it didn't matter; Squamiset had already managed to shuck his bindings and stagger to his feet. With a quick deft motion he swiped the cutlass from Hooker's hand, and the fires faded almost as quickly as they'd begun.

Hooker, furious, had regained his senses. Rockingham came up behind him and handed him his own sword. The mercenary swished the weapon appraisingly through the air a few times, his red face resuming the grim death-giving cast it had worn before Squamiset's fires. Despite the beating that the old man had taken, he appeared to be in possession of himself, and as the blades cut through the air and rang out against each other Will saw that Squamiset was surprisingly adept at swordplay. His ability to fight back caught Hooker by surprise. As if by communal instinct the crowd pulled back, making space on the foredeck for the duel.

Squamiset was quite athletic for his age, and he must have learned how to use a sword during his exile in England. Unfortunately, Hooker was a lifelong soldier of fortune, and his skills were an order of magnitude more advanced. His movements were blunt and economical—no spins or flourishes—but he parried the old man's thrusts and slashes effortlessly, and it quickly became obvious how the fight would end. Hooker mounted his attack patiently, backing Squamiset against the bulwark of the forecastle. Will groaned, bracing himself for bloodshed. But Squamiset still had tricks to play. He swung the cutlass in a wide figure eight, and the blade seemed to multiply, tripling and quadrupling until the air space separating him from the militia captain was an impenetrable whir of fast-moving steel.

Hooker stepped back, looking for an opening. He aimed the

Governor's sword, making ready for a killing thrust. But suddenly Squamiset's whirring field of cutlasses became one blade again, and in a single downward stroke it cleaved off Hooker's right hand, sending it thumping down the deck, twitching and clenching like a small creature with a life of its own. Hooker blanched and dropped to his knees. With his left hand he grasped the stump of his right, which, for a moment, spurted through his fingers in a radiating fountain of blood.

A shocked silence descended on the ship. High above on the main-mast, John Rockingham's scarlet pennant snapped in the wind. A small, bent, wiry man—the ship's surgeon, Will thought—stepped forward to wrap white-faced Hooker's arm and then led him cursing loudly below decks. A boy around Will's age—the surgeon's assistant, he presumed—bent to pick up the bloody hand from the deck, flinching as it clenched one final time of its own accord. Green with disgust, the boy wrapped the hand in waxed sailcloth and hurried down the hatch after the surgeon.

Meanwhile, Squamiset's eyes met Will's. *Follow your instincts. Continue the journey. Don't forget what I have taught you.*

In the next moment the old man sprang up onto the cathead and launched himself forward, clearing the bowsprit to knife headfirst into the heaving swells.

Rockingham, scarlet with fury, screamed an order. A scramble ensued as militiamen loaded their muskets and blunderbusses and lined up at the rail. Squamiset broke the surface fifty yards to starboard. He was naked to the waist, lean and wiry, his wet silver hair trailing down his back over the network of red welts from Hooker's cutlass. As Will had seen, he was a swift swimmer, looking calm and purposeful as he put distance between himself and the frigate. A loud popping shook the air as the Governor's militiamen stippled the water with balls and buckshot, exclaiming with vengeful joy at this unexpected opportunity for shooting practice—and with such a notorious demon as the target.

For a moment Will lost sight of Squamiset in the choppy water and splashing musket balls. Not daring to breathe, he scanned the surface of the ocean. After a moment he finally spotted him, but what he saw only broke his heart. Squamiset's body floated loose-limbed on the swells, the great blade of a nose pointing senselessly up at the sky. The old man's pale throat and part of his chest broke the surface, and the flesh was ripped by multiple wounds—little rosebuds where buckshot had punctured the flesh, horrid flowering carnations from high-impact lead balls. The water surrounding him was dyed crimson with his blood.

Will's last glimpse of Squamiset took place in one fractured instant, as the guards propelled him across the quarterdeck toward the hatch leading down to the brig, just before a wave rose up to swallow the old man beneath the surface. Horrifyingly, Will had also seen half a dozen shark fins glistening menacingly amidst the choppy swells and a bird, a shearwater, perhaps, or an osprey, flying low above the blood-stained surface.

Eighteen

Chained to the floor in the low-ceilinged space between the frigate's decks, Will stared up into the cramped darkness and struggled to calm his breathing. His right ankle was imprisoned by a heavy manacle attached to an iron ring bolted to the decking, and a short section of chain linked the iron cuffs around his wrists. At first he had tested the chains by struggling against them, but all this accomplished was to redouble the pain where his skin was already raw from the abrasive manila cords.

In part he welcomed the pain. He could scarcely believe what his own eyes had seen. He'd underestimated Rockingham's cruelty. And the result was that Squamiset was dead. Will had been left to confront his fate alone.

He wondered if the Governor already had detailed plans for the execution. He wondered if he would catch one last glimpse of his childhood home or if they would keep a hood over his head as they marched him to the common. Young Will Poole, the citizens of New Meadow would say, shaking their heads. Such a pity. A promising young life ended so prematurely. But that's what comes, other voices would grimly intone, of choosing to consort with the Devil.

Maybe this is all only a dream, he thought. Maybe I'll wake up under the furs on the sleeping platform of our little hut on the island, with a crackling fire and the reassuring roar of breakers in the distance. Maybe I'll sit up, stretch my arms, sip a bit of herb-scented water from the clay bowl, and share a warm corn cake with Natoncks and Squamiset and my beautiful, sad-eyed Shambisqua. But no. Such comforts were far beyond reach now, and thinking about them only made him feel worse. The only thing he could truly look forward to now was a quick end to his misery. Taking several deep breaths in an effort to calm himself, he remembered the old dreams of flying. The more you *wished* to fly, the less likely it was that you could. So he tried to forget where he was. He tried to erase from his mind everything that had happened.

Come to me, duck. I need your wings and your golden eyes. He peered up into the darkness, but all he could see was Squamiset's face. That remarkable curving nose. The laugh lines in the leathery skin around his eyes and mouth. The amused friendliness in his expression. That look of serenity and blank distraction that came over him when he lay on the ground to rest or think or search for visions. All this, gone forever.

What a skill it would be to simply ignore your thoughts. To lie on the ground and watch them fly overhead like migrating geese. Not to think. Just to be.

He dozed and regained consciousness, still alone, still chained to the iron ring on the floor in the inky blackness between the frigate's decks. In the next moment he found himself pounding on the planks above his head, shouting at the top of his lungs to be heard through the decking: "I have something to say! I wish to see John Rockingham!" He paused a moment. "I confess! I abjure the savage religion! Tell the Governor I am reborn to the Truth!"

The guards came down with keys to release his ankle chain from the iron ring. They led him up the ladder—he stumbled a few times on the way up, a poor lost soul unbalanced by the urgency of repenting—and into the blinding light. When his eyes adjusted, he noted that it was a bright day only by contrast with the cavelike gloom between decks. Purple storm clouds packed the horizon, and a cold northeast wind licked the ocean to the texture of hammered steel. Perhaps the frigate would be delayed in its journey back to New Meadow. A strong gale, if it came, could easily blow them off course. But Will knew he couldn't count on the weather to do his bidding.

In the master's cabin, John Rockingham and James Overlock sat with their elbows resting on the narrow table and their backs to the windows overlooking the grey-green ocean with its foreboding purple horizon. They watched him as the guards led him in: Rockingham with undisguised distaste, Overlock with a more complex array of emotions—hatred tempered by fear, perhaps, and maybe even a vestige of friendly concern. Hooker was not present; Will assumed he was still in the sick bay. At Will's back, the loyal crewmen who'd brought him up from the brig stood guard. The room was tense with expectation.

He took a deep breath and sank to his knees. Tears streamed freely from his eyes; he was shaken and remorseful. "I abjure," he repeated in a small, miserable voice. "I wish to be welcomed back to the Truth."

Rockingham eyed him with a deeply suspicious gaze. Overlock gave him an encouraging nod.

"If I must die," Will continued, "I am willing to accept my fate. But I do not want to burn in Hell for eternity. I see now that everything I've done has been selfish and wrong. I see now that I have been led astray by Satan, who has encouraged me to turn my back on the true Lord of Creation. Please, Your Excellency. I throw myself upon your mercy. And His."

There was a long silence in the master's cabin. The hull creaked, and the sailcloth snapped in the wind. Out on the quarterdeck a cleaning detachment broke into song. Beyond the row of diamond-paned windows the ship traced a wavering line across the troubled, steely ocean. "May God grant you the mercy you seek," Rockingham finally said. Beside him, Overlock let out his breath, whether from relief or disappointment it was not quite clear. The Governor cleared his throat. "The savage who tempted you is dead, Will, as you have seen. But the evil he has wrought persists—in the world at large, and in you. We cannot forget this dangerous fact, but for the moment let's put it aside. Do you hereby swear, upon your immortal soul, to reject all heathen beliefs from this moment forward and until your dying breath, and to embrace the Truth as revealed to the world in the New Testament by Jesus Christ, the Son of God?"

Will waited a moment, pretending to consider it, then nodded. "I do."

"Do you promise to dedicate yourself to the task of uncovering that Truth in your every waking moment for as long as you live and breathe?"

Will blinked. "I do so promise, Your Excellency. I shall try my hardest."

There was another long silence as Rockingham and Overlock savored their respective victories. As Will understood it, his change of heart was the best possible outcome for both of them. For the Governor, it was proof that the attraction of life among the savages was but a cruel delusion, a Satanic trick designed to lure gullible citizens away from the Truth. In debt for his very life, Will would become New Meadow's best living example of the power of Christian redemption.

For Overlock, the matter was more personal. Of course he was happy to be proven right and was smugly satisfied to see Will brought up short. But the former steward wasn't completely heartless. Deep down, Will knew, he possessed a lingering sense of loyalty to Thomas Poole and to the family he'd spent most of his adult life serving. Moreover, his fortunes were secure by now; his position close by Rockingham's side was evidence enough of that. And he'd probably never relished the idea of seeing Will put to death.

"Unlock him," Rockingham ordered.

"Thank you, Excellency," Will said with the most abject humility, staring at the floor. He held up his wrists for one of the guards while another knelt to unlock the manacle around his ankle.

"Remember your newfound purpose, Will," Rockingham instructed. "It is not I whom you should thank but our merciful and all-powerful Lord."

Will nodded with all the reverent zealousness of a new convert. Once the manacles were off, he got to his feet and concentrated on generating an illusion he'd dreamed up in the darkness of the brig. It was a colossal black demon with fiery red eyes, spiraling ram's horns, and a ferocious, bearlike muzzle. So tall it had to hunch down in the low-ceilinged cabin, the demon leaned forward to rest its warty talons on the table. It opened its jaws to display long, sharp yellow teeth set in angry scarlet gums and let out a roar that shook the cabin windows. Overlock shrank back, raising his arms to fend the creature off. Rockingham sprang to his feet, pale and stony-faced, his high-backed chair toppling to the floor. The guards were momentarily frozen in place, torn between their duty and their instinct to flee. Unfortunately, Will could not sustain the illusion long enough. It flickered and faded, leaving him roaring comically with his hands grasping the edge of the table.

Rockingham bent down to recover his chair. The guards started laughing, and Overlock, after a moment, laughed along with them. Ears burning with humiliation, Will understood that he'd now doomed himself irrevocably. There would be no more Christian mercy from the Governor after this. He lunged for the nearest guard's sword, grasping the handle and jerking it toward the ceiling. The weapon rang out as it slid from its scabbard, a high steady note, and suddenly time slowed down. Will's own movements felt ponderous, as if he were swimming through molasses, but the others in the room were slower; it was as if they were frozen in a dream. Will ran for the door. A quick-thinking guard stepped into his path, and Will lowered his shoulder and knocked the man aside. But Rockingham had already moved across the cabin, spreading his arms to block the door.

Will raised the sword. "Move aside, Your Excellency, or I swear by the Manitoo that I will kill you."

Rockingham stared at him, and for a moment it looked as if he would dare Will to try it. But he must have seen something in Will's eyes that gave him pause. He stepped aside, and Will ran past him out the door. "Stop him!" the Governor cried out. The words sounded deep and slow in the background, as if they were coming from a different world or a different dimension.

Will slammed the door shut behind him before the guards could reach it. Time had speeded up again, and he didn't have much of it left. He sprinted up the stairs to the quarterdeck, and a group of crewmen who'd been scrubbing the decking sprang up to bar his path. He feinted one direction and dove the other, rolling across the planks to evade their grasping arms. He sprinted along the gangway to the forecastle with its high taffarel. Without pausing he vaulted over it, clearing the beakhead and the figurehead as he plummeted feet first into the cold green sea.

Nineteen

He awoke with the hot sun burning his face, his heels immersed in a tranquil surf, and a mouth as dry as charred shoe leather. With great effort, he pushed himself up to a sitting position and looked around. He'd washed ashore on a small beach walled in on three sides by a kind of dense vegetation that he didn't recognize. A slow-moving stream flowed into the gently lapping sea. Dizzy, he collapsed back onto the sand. Let them come, he thought. Only first give me a moment to die.

When he came to again he felt a bit stronger. The sun was lower in the sky, it was cooler, and from the length of the shadows he judged it was around four o'clock in the afternoon. A flock of terns, half a dozen grey and white birds the size of small gulls with jaunty black crests, stood vigil on the beach. All were facing the same direction, into the steady breeze blowing in off the sea, and each watched him with the same disapproving sidelong gaze. "Are you Manitoo?" he croaked.

The birds didn't answer but kept a close watch on him. The sand was sugary and warm on his salt-caked heels and shoulders. His body ached, and his throat was so dry that he could barely swallow. There were festering sores where the manacles had chafed and bruised his wrists and ankle, but he was alive. That was something.

Despite his physical discomfort, he felt a strange compulsion to explain himself to the birds. "It looks like I'm free. But my friend is dead, and I have nowhere to go." The terns watched him, judgmental and suspicious. He flapped his arms, and the birds flew off in unison, veering away from him as if they shared a single, decisive mind. They soared away down the beach in perfect formation, letting out high-pitched shrieks. They were lovely birds: sleek cloud-grey wingbacks; snow-white tails forked like amberjacks.

He crawled over to the edge of the freshwater stream. Dropping to his elbows, he cupped his hands in the tea-colored water and brought it to his lips. It tasted of mud and peat moss, but he was too thirsty to care. He lowered his face to gulp directly from the stream. This much he knew: he could never go back to the New England settlements. Rockingham was like a spider at the center of a web of influence. Even when the spider was gone, the web would still be there, and other men of ambition would scurry in to take control of it. If Will's true identity were ever discovered, the authorities would make sure that his crimes were punished.

No doubt the men on the frigate assumed that he was dead. He'd plunged into the ocean many miles from shore; Overlock knew that Will could barely swim. How he'd survived at all was a mystery to him. He had vague memories of holding his breath and kicking downward through the green depths, following the receding profile of the swimming duck. Perhaps it had been a hallucination or perhaps it had not, but by some miracle he'd returned to the surface far from the frigate. He'd come across a piece of driftwood, a slick black log with the remnants of a root ball attached, and he'd draped himself across it to stay afloat. After who knew how many hours of floating he'd lost consciousness, and he'd woken up on the beach.

The noise of insects coming from the forest was strident and angry-sounding. Perhaps he was dead after all. Perhaps this beach was Purgatory, the gateway to Hell. He took off his tattered canvas breeches and waded into the stream to rinse the salt from his skin. Just as he was about to dunk himself, he caught a glimpse of something in the shadows across the slow-moving current. Heart racing, he splashed back up to the dry beach. Now he could see it clearly: a symmetrical, warty, loglike creature lurking at the edge of the stilt-rooted bushes. Two large reptilian eyes protruded above the water, watching him carefully.

Shuddering, he pulled on the salt-starched breeches, and a callused hand clapped his shoulder. He wheeled around with an involuntary yelp, expecting to see Hooker or Overlock or one of Rockingham's men. But it was a local Indian, tall and straight and covered from head to foot in a layer of cracked reddish mud. Behind him stood several others, all covered in the same dried mud. Some wore pendants fashioned from Spanish doubloons. Will recognized the coins because Zeke had shown him one that he'd brought back from a trading voyage; even from a distance he could make out old King Philip's arrogant profile in the burnished gold.

He held up a hand and spoke a greeting in Algonkian. The Indians stared uncomprehendingly, and it became clear that they did not speak that language. The one who had touched his shoulder reached out to grasp his forearm, and Will, alarmed, stepped back out of his way. The man shook his head and raised his hand in a gesture of friendship. It seemed that these strangers intended him no harm. In the end, seeing no other alternative, Will followed them into the trees.

They walked along the banks of the stream through a forest alive with exotic squawks and chirrups and a strange repeating call that sounded like a whipsaw. Strangely colored birds exploded out of the greenery to alight in swaying branches and on broad waxy leaves that Will did not recognize. Inland from the sea breezes the air was close and muggy. In the shade of this strange forest the stream was obsidian black. A scent like spruce or fir mingled with the earthy odor of rotting peat. He felt light-headed and disoriented. Thirsty again, he knelt beside the stream to drink, but one of the Indians put a hand on his shoulder and shook his head. This man passed him a gourd, and Will drank deeply from it.

They came to a flooded forest: hundreds of trees stood with their feet in water that reflected the deep blue sky. Near the bank, a huge dead tree trunk rose out of the water like a sun-silvered obelisk. Crowning the trunk was a gigantic bird's nest, a messy tangle of reeds and sticks. Three young ospreys peered down out of it, the bright feathers on their heads ruffled by the breeze. Will felt as if he were walking through a dream.

Dusk came as they marched into the Indians' village. Will felt hollow and exhausted. The men led him down a path through the center of the village to an outlying *wetu* (these people called it a *chickee*, he later discovered) made of bent saplings and thickly matted reeds. They gestured for Will to enter and abruptly left him. Inside, he waited for his eyes to adjust. There was no fire and little light. After a moment he discovered that he was not alone. Seated cross-legged on the sandy floor was a bedraggled, elderly figure wrapped in a glossy black pelt that Will imagined might have come from a jaguar. He thought perhaps this hut was the local version of an almshouse, a dwelling place for slaves and castaways.

He stood in the shadows, unsure of what to do. He craved the chance to lie down on the cool sand and rest his bones, but he didn't wish to be disrespectful to this old stranger. A patch of red-gold twilight slanted in through the smoke hole, piercing the gloom a bit, but it wasn't enough to reveal the figure's face. The old man's or old woman's head was inclined as if the stranger was deep in thought, and the face was hidden by a mass of tangled white hair. "Forgive me, old one," he said in Algonkian. "May I sit?"

The ancient being raised its head. The face was gaunt and wrinkled and marred by scabs, but the eyes were so shockingly familiar that Will lost his balance and tumbled backward onto the ground.

"What cheer, Will," Squamiset said. "It is good to see that you are come, though I must admit I expected you a bit sooner."

"But I saw you shot to pieces! How can you not be dead?"

Squamiset's eyes glinted in the twilight. He looked older to Will, and frailer, yet the familiar amused look in his eyes was as welcome as a crackling fire on a chilly February afternoon. "As you yourself have seen,

Will," he said after a moment, "it is no great trick to cause people to see that which they most desire, or that which they most dread."

Will lowered himself back on his elbows, groaning with relief. "Well, I knew you were casting illusions on the decks of the frigate, with the fires and the many-bladed cutlass. But those musket shots were well aimed, and there were so many men shooting. And I saw shark fins. I was sure I'd seen you die."

The old man glanced down at his arms and his crossed legs. "And yet, clearly, you had not."

Will shook his head. He was too exhausted to argue. It was enough that Squamiset was alive and that they were together once more. Letting his mind relax, he settled his head back on the cool sand and closed his eyes.

Twenty

In all they spent eleven days in the village. On the seventh day, accompanied by a group of local youths, Squamiset used his knife to mark a tall pine. They built a blazing fire and banked coals around the base of the tree to weaken it. They chopped into the cinders with heavy flint hand axes, and the pine careened to the forest floor with a great crackling *whoosh*. They used scallop shells to strip away the bark and packed wet clay along the sides and ends of the log to keep the wood from burning as they shoveled live coals along its centerline. Little by little the embers ate into the heartwood, and they scooped the burnt wood and dying embers out with shells and chisels fashioned from beaver teeth. When the groove was clean, they shoveled in another batch of embers. This process was repeated over the course of three days until the log was hollow and they had the hull of a dugout. It was oddly light for an object so large: without too much strain Will and Squamiset alone could carry it. When the bottom was scraped smooth and oiled, Squamiset carved a beautiful new version of his osprey design on the prow. Will used a beaver-tooth chisel to carve his own design on the stern, a flying duck viewed from the side with one wide, all-seeing eye.

The night before the travelers planned to depart, the villagers gave them a feast. There was singing and dancing. Food and tobacco were offered to bless the journey and give thanks to the Manitoo for the bounties of the earth. Squamiset entertained the gathering by causing the fire to rear up in flickering illusions: eagles, bears, writhing serpents, fanciful monsters, and detailed reproductions of the castles and cathedrals he'd visited during his exile in Spain and England. In the morning a sweat lodge was prepared to cleanse the two travelers for their journey. Afterward Will and Squamiset bathed in a crystalline pool that bubbled up from a limestone sinkhole encircled by tall pines. Then it was time to go. Even loaded with provisions—smoked fish and shellfish, nuts, fresh and dried fruits, water gourds, and several reed baskets filled to the brim with parched corn—the *mishoon* floated high and true on the tea-colored river. Local children ran along the riverbanks to wish them well. Where the river met the sea, the travelers raised their paddles in a final salute, and the children sent them off with a chorus of owl-like hooting.

The ocean was calm, brushed by a light northwesterly breeze, and the sky was clear. It was a fine day for paddling. Will found himself more pleased than worried to be charting a course for new adventures. When they were far enough out to avoid any trouble that might be awaiting them along shore, they pointed the slender dugout southward. According to Squamiset's reckoning, they had at least two weeks of paddling in front of them before the southwest passage opened up. Then they would steer toward Sowwaniu, the home of Cautántowwit, Bringer of Seeds.

Weeks went by. They paddled during the day and slept in hammocks beside windswept beaches at night. As the provisions dwindled, they began to subsist more and more on the fish and fruit and coconuts that they harvested ashore. Squamiset would never admit it, but Will could tell by the set of his shoulders that he was growing tired. His hair, which he no longer bothered to braid, had turned more white than silver, and it was wispier than before, like feathery clouds on a winter day. Yet his mind was as sharp as ever, and he appeared content to be underway on this long foretold journey.

The mainland beaches ended, and they were able to alter their bearing to the southwest into a calm tropical sea. One afternoon they came within view of a small, apparently uninhabited island. The dugout floated in translucent green water above a white sand bottom. A few hundred yards ahead the water darkened to midnight blue, indicating a deep channel. Beyond that was a thin strip of white sand beach backed by a fringe of storm-tattered palms and mangroves. In every other direction the sea stretched out in incandescent green shallows, with schools of bonefish patrolling the sand bottom like furtive white-on-white ghosts. A warm southwesterly wind rippled the surface. They'd been paddling into it for days, a moist air fragrant with sea smells and unfamiliar blossoms. Squamiset laid his paddle across the hull and leaned back with his arms spread out, tilting his face to the sky.

"Everything all right?" Will asked.

"We're nearly there, Will." The old man's voice was odd: thin and breathless and tinged with something that sounded like wonder.

"Almost where, Squamiset?"

"Sowwaniu." He raised his paddle and pointed it at the hurricane-wrecked island beyond the deep channel.

"I don't think so. The Spanish treasure ports are still to the southwest of us: New Providence, Portobelo, Cartagena. Maybe beyond those—"

"No, Will." The old man held up a trembling hand. "Sowwaniu is *here*. We have arrived at the home of Cautántowwit. Paddle quickly, for I feel myself weakening."

Filled with new anxiety, Will dug into the limpid water with his paddle. The island seemed to recede before them even as they approached it, and it felt like hours—though it was really only minutes—before the dugout made it across the deep channel and nosed up to the white sand beach.

Squamiset got unsteadily to his feet. He stepped out onto the sand, stumbled with uncharacteristic clumsiness, recovered, and without a further word set off at a lope into the tangled vegetation. Will tried to remain calm. He called out Squamiset's name, but the old man didn't seem to hear. In the next moment Will lost sight of him.

He dragged the dugout up onto the beach and strode into the jungle. Squamiset had not taken the usual precautions to conceal his path; it was all too easy to track him. Almost immediately a cloud of mosquitoes descended. Will scratched compulsively at his exposed face and neck, his bare arms and ankles. The vegetation was interlaced with vines and thorny brambles. The old man's lack of care had itself been an artifice: after following his trail in four separate directions, Will understood that he'd been tricked.

Other than the insistent whine of the mosquitoes, there was no sound in the overgrown interior of the island. No footfalls, no distant crack from a broken twig. His gut told Will that he was alone. Terribly, irrevocably alone.

His face and eyes had begun to swell, and the individual mosquito bites had combined into a singular intolerable burning itchiness over all his exposed skin. It was no good swatting at his arms and legs, though he kept doing it. He looked around desperately for a direct path back to the sea. Finding none, he ran blindly toward where he thought he would find the beach, a headlong, panicked flight through the jungle without regard for the roots and vines that tripped him up or the stinging thorns that lacerated him.

After the relief of immersing himself in the bathlike seawater, he stood dripping by the dugout. It was just as he'd left it, except that now Squamiset's bundle had disappeared. Will could find no footprints but his own in the white sand. It was as if his old friend had never existed.

Twenty-One

The old man floated on his back in the clear and pleasantly lukewarm water, gazing up at the blue sky. He had done it. He had reached the home of Cautántowwit, Bringer of Seeds, where there was no strife, no want, no warfare, no disease. He understood now that Sowwaniu could have been anywhere. It was not the location in itself but the path taken to get there—not the existence of peace and plentiful harvests, of health and love and harmony among all creatures but the act of striving to reach them that mattered. This was the lesson of Sowwaniu. He did not know if Will had understood it. He hoped so.

High above the old man the osprey circled. It rode the wind currents, adjusting its wings minimally, sometimes plunging downward with exhilarating speed, sometimes rising up on a plume of warm air, always tracing a slow, meditative circle in the sky, a circle with no beginning and no end. There came a moment when the osprey folded its wings and dove. In the same instant, the old man's spirit left his body and flew up to meet the diving bird. The two spirits became one, and then the sky was empty.

Epilogue

When the first group of English settlers landed on the island in 1659, they were surprised by the size of the native population. On the mainland, most of the remaining Indian villages were too shattered and demoralized to constitute meaningful barriers to English settlement, but that wasn't the case here. Fortunately, the local Wampanoags did not have warlike spirits, and they were willing to negotiate. There were only eighteen Englishmen in this first wave—Baptist sheep farmers for the most part, fleeing the intolerant Puritans who had come to dominate Massachusetts Bay and much of the rest of New England. The Baptists negotiated the rights to a parcel of land around a small harbor on the island's northwestern shore and went about the hard work of establishing a colony.

It was only later, after they'd survived those difficult first months, that the new settlers began to wonder how certain things about the island had come to pass. How had these isolated Indians learned so many words of English? How had they come to understand enough about English common law to insist, in those first negotiations, upon establishing a system to regulate the settlers' grazing rights? It was puzzling, but the Englishmen were too prudent to ask many questions. The truth was—as had been the case elsewhere in New England—that the help of the native population was critical to the new settlers' survival. Why risk angering their hosts, they reasoned, when everything was going so well?

After a few years, with the tiny English colony showing every sign of prospering, the sheep farmers sent for their families. But there were whisperings of strange and uncanny events. The most persistent rumors centered on an Indian sorcerer who had a habit of wandering alone across the island's fog-shrouded moors. No one had ever seen him up close but had only glimpsed him from a distance. One colonist, chasing an escaped lamb over the moors, thought he saw this lone walker, but as he drew near, the figure became a deer and bounded off into the scrub. Others reported approaching a seated figure only to discover a man-shaped rock or bush where they had imagined the figure to be. It was said that this mysterious islander had once been an Englishman. It was said that he could appear and disappear at will. It was said that he could make trees talk, create strange apparitions out of living flame, and even fly by simply casting himself up into the air and taking wing.

As is the case with many such stories, the details became exaggerated with each telling, and as time went on, fewer and fewer people actually believed them. Eventually they became the sort of story told around a winter hearth to impress upon young children the importance of not wandering off by themselves. It was inevitable, of course—then, now, always—that a few children *did* wander off. And that is how this story came to be.

THE END

Author's Note

"Unless we can find some way to understand the reality of mythic thinking, we remain prisoners of our own language, our own thoughtworld. In our world one story is real, the other, fantasy. In the Indian way of thinking both stories are true because they describe personal experience. Historical events happened once and are gone forever. Mythic events return like the swans of spring . . . They are essential truths, not contingent ones."
        —Robin Ridington

Will Poole's Island takes place during a period in history that is, for many Americans, overshadowed by the Thanksgiving legend on one end and the patriotic triumph of 1776 on the other. My ancestors arrived in New England in the Great Migration of the 1630s and became some of the earliest English settlers of the region we now call Connecticut. I also have Indian ancestors, and a desire to learn more about both groups is what led me back to the seventeenth century. One of the things that caused me to linger there was the sense that some basic truths about the period are missing from our national mythology: the horror of a mostly unintentional but unquestionably convenient genocide, and the clash between two very different worldviews that were nonetheless both rooted in the visionary and the unseen.

Although the novel doesn't focus on actual historical personalities, events in its main characters' stories are drawn in part from the experiences of real people. The most obvious inspiration for the character of Squamiset is Tisquantum (Squanto), who was kidnapped along with twenty-seven others in 1614 and sold as a slave in Málaga. Like Squamiset, Tisquantum escaped Spain and ended up in England; he eventually made his way back to America to become an interpreter for the Puritans of the Plimoth Plantation in their negotiations with various Algonkian-speaking groups. But Tisquantum was not the only New England Indian who was kidnapped, enslaved, and/or carried back to Europe as a curiosity. As early as 1501, Gaspar Corte Real abducted fifty Algonkian speakers on the coast of what would later become Maine. In 1523, Giovanni de Verrazzano observed the smoke of bonfires along the New England coast. He met Indians "as beautiful of stature and build as I can possibly describe" and took an eight-year-old boy as a souvenir. In 1611, Edward Harlow took six Wampanoag prisoners on Cape Cod, one of whom, Epenow, was "shown up and down London for money as a wonder." And so on. These are the incidents that made it into the historical record. We can assume there were more.

The character of Will Poole may also be less of an aberration than he seems. Written history (slanted as it is by those doing the writing) provides more than one example of breakaway Englishmen punished severely for going to live among Indians. Moreover, there were many English children in New England and Canada who were kidnapped and adopted into Indian communities. These young people were often discovered to be most reluctant, upon their rescue or ransom, to rejoin a society they'd come to view as repressive and overly strict.

Regarding the minor characters, Captain Hooker shares some of the background and personality of Myles Standish, who led a preemptive massacre on the Wessagusset band in 1623 and placed the head of one victim, an alleged conspirator, on a pike above the New Plimoth palisade. Some (though of course not all) seventeenth-century Puritan leaders, like the fictional Governor Rockingham, did seem to be motivated by a baleful mix of piety, worldly ambition, and cruelty. Three of my Connecticut ancestors—whose well-preserved graves can still be viewed in the crypt of the Center Church on the Green in New Haven—were swindled out of their fortune by a grasping household servant.

But in the end these real-life figures were merely inspirations for a wholly invented narrative. *Will Poole's Island* is a fictional tale, pure and simple, although I can't resist the observation that the moment-by-moment reality of "true" history (as opposed to its bullet-pointed outline) is equally unknowable, and therefore just as speculative.

The basic layout of the walled village of New Meadow has something in common with early New Haven, but it could also stand in for many of the mid-seventeenth-century English settlements along the Connecticut, Rhode Island, and Massachusetts coasts. In a similar vein, the Indian villages featured in the novel are meant to serve as plausible re-creations rather than specific historical sites. Some will recognize Nantucket in the remote island that provides a safe haven for Will, Squamiset, and Natoncks. Indeed, due to its position far out to sea and its dangerous shoals, Nantucket did avoid English settlement until 1659—quite late in the game as far as the colonization of coastal New England goes. The island's large Wampanoag population remained, for a time, untouched by the European diseases that decimated most of the mainland communities.

A quick word about place names and Indian population groups. "Indian" is the term preferred by many contemporary Native Americans and is therefore used throughout the book. "Algonkian" is a word I use throughout the book to describe a language family, a group that included, among others, the Wampanoag, Narragansett, Massachusett, and Pequot peoples. Within this larger category, "Wampanoag" ("People of the Eastern Light" or "Dawnlanders") refers to various related groups living in the area around Cape Cod and the islands of Martha's Vineyard and Nantucket. It should be remembered that in and before the seventeenth century these people were unlikely to have called themselves by that name; they might have referred to themselves by the name of their specific locale ("Mannomoyik"; "Nauset") or by some other designation. It's interesting to note that for American Indian groups in general, the currently used names were often bestowed by neighboring groups, many of them rivals or enemies.

In seventeenth-century English usage, spelling had yet to be set in stone; the ongoing process of regularization was not complete until the publication of Samuel Johnson's dictionary in 1755. This is another reason that documents of the time are so fascinating to read. A writer could spell however he wanted, depending upon how the words sounded to his ear and, presumably, upon his mood and aesthetic instinct. When it comes to *Indian* words—which were based not on a written alphabet at all but on the phonetic interpretation of the English listener—the variations in spelling were even more pronounced. For the most part, I relied upon Roger Williams's excellent *Key into the Language of America*, first published in London in 1643, but on occasion I found myself indulging in my own version of period reenactment: modifying spellings to better represent my personal interpretation of the phonetic speech of the novel's characters.

In researching and writing this book, it has been my deeply held intention to honor the original peoples of America, some of whom I am lucky enough to count as my ancestors. I have done my best to represent their dwelling places, their lifeways, and their spiritual beliefs as accurately as possible; however, I have found that the exigencies and limitations of a fictional narrative call for the occasional use of poetic license. Together with my own investigative and imaginative failings, this means that some inaccuracies and misconceptions have inevitably crept in, and for this I apologize.

As to the story's "magical" elements, anyone researching seventeenth-century America is bound to be struck by the realization that in the firsthand documents penned by Europeans of the time, factual events often receive the same emphasis and are reported in the same breath as those we would now consider fantasy. Hard-bitten seafarers were always spotting mermaids, tritons, and sea serpents; heretical Puritan women were believed to have given birth to strange hybrid monsters; a comet appearing over Europe in 1618 was believed to portend a climactic battle between Good and Evil. And then of course there are the well-documented collective obsessions with Satan and witchcraft. I took this tendency, together with the perspective on the Indian worldview expressed in Robin Ridington's quote above, as guiding wisdom for a storyteller. Who's to say what the actual reality was?

My profound gratitude goes out to Joseph Monninger, Jack Hodgkins, Ernest Hebert, Robert Redick, and K.L. Going for their generous and insightful early readings. Jonathan Perry and others at the Wampanoag Indigenous Program at Plimoth Plantation were instrumental in introducing me to the elusive realities of seventeenth-century America, as were the employees and volunteers of the New Haven Colony Historical Society, the Center Church on the Green in New Haven, the Plimoth Plantation, the Nantucket Historical Association, the Nantucket Whaling Museum, the Mashantucket Pequot Museum and Research Center, and the Wampanoag Tribe of Gay Head Aquinnah Cultural Center. I am indebted to the brilliant historical writings of Nathaniel Philbrick of Nantucket and to Stephen Roxburgh for his patient, perceptive, and exacting editorial guidance. The book would not have been possible at all without the long-term support of Reb and Daintry Jensen, the best in-laws a writer could hope for, or the inspiration and example of Chuck Weed and Susan Edwards Wing, who have never wavered in their unconditional love. Finally, my deepest love and gratitude to Julie, Roo, and Toby, whose encouragement and cheerful self-sufficiency have allowed me to embark upon this and many other adventures. You are my beacons.

54823945R00112

Made in the USA
Charleston, SC
13 April 2016